T0069243

Karolinum Press

ABOUT THE AUTHOR

Vladislav Vančura (1891–1942) was an author, playwright, and pioneer of the Czech avant-garde, along with being a member of the resistance during the Second World War.

He was a founder and leader of the influential artistic collective Devětsil. A Communist from 1921 until 1929 (when he was expelled from the party), he remained a leftist for the rest of his life. As a member of the Czech resistance under the Nazi occupation, Vančura headed the writers' section of the National Revolutionary Intelligence Committee. In 1942 he was executed by the SS in the reprisals for the assassination of Reinhard Heydrich.

A highly influential author in his homeland, Vančura's creative work is influenced as much by Expressionism and his experiences in the First World War as by cinematography and the concept of Poetism, a movement he helped formulate with Devětsil; his writing spans the spectrum from social protest, such as *Baker Jan Marhoul* and *Fields of Plough, Fields of War*, to poetic and humorous works like *Summer of Caprice* and the Czech children's classic *Kubula and Kuba Kubikula*.

Humor is fundamental to Vančura's style, yet in each of his works it manifests itself differently, as subtle irony, parody, linguistic experimentation, and even "new methods of expression."

Because of his extensive work in theater and film, Vančura's literary works incorporate a number of dramatic and cinematic elements. This is perhaps one reason why his novels have been adapted so successfully for the screen. 1967 saw the release of two classic films based on Vančura's work: *Capricious Summer*, directed by Jiří Menzel, is perhaps the most charming movie to come out of the Czechoslovak New Wave, while František Vláčil's version of *Marketa Lazarová*, Vančura's experimental and brutal historical novel, is the most critically acclaimed film in Czech cinema.

MODERN CZECH CLASSICS

Vladislav Vančura
Summer of Caprice

Translation from the Czech by Mark Corner

KAROLINUM PRESS 2016

KAROLINUM PRESS
Karolinum Press is a publishing department
of Charles University
Ovocný trh 5/560, 116 36 Prague 1
Czech Republic
www.karolinum.cz

Translation © 2016 by Mark Corner
Epilogue © 2016 by Jan Rubeš

Cover illustration by Jiří Grus
Designed by Zdeněk Ziegler
Set and printed in the Czech Republic
by Karolinum Press

Cataloging-in-Publication Data is available
from the National Library of the Czech Republic

ISBN 978-80-246-3289-6 (pbk)
ISBN 978-80-246-1195-3 (hbk)
ISBN 978-80-246-3367-1 (ebk)

Many daredevil characters, fetched up at the start of the magnificent month of June, find their hardened features smoothed over as they sit in the shade of the plane trees. See how the branches and the high column of mercury rise and fall like the diaphragm of a sleeper. See the swaying of the sunshade and set your eyes upon that face, once so repugnant. Let them rest in peace, that nose and swollen lip which have erupted so violently from the face, let them grow calm because, for goodness' sake, this is a time of quiet for the town.

In the midst of fertile fields there are plenty of white farmsteads as imagined by our national poetry. The young bulls have become oxen, the heifers are with calf and May has passed on.

Should you be able to do so, dress in white and venture hesitantly into a seat in front of your hotel. Great Scott! Is the example of our forefathers not good enough? On went their belts, over their arms went their coats and one step at a time they edged their way towards the orchards below, where a stool was already prepared for them to sit on.

In those days the camp followers, decked in bonnets and sporting flat and well-ventilated shoes, the sort that didn't dig up the ground, used to move from man to man, from stool to stool, extracting invoice pads from deep and bulging pockets, tearing off one slip after another. A pink flush spread to the tufts of their noses whenever they spoke to a guest saying:

"Good day, sir. Isn't it a beautiful morning? Don't you enjoy a moment like this, as the chime of ten comes flying down from the time-honoured tower of St. Lawrence's Basilica? We believe that there's nothing more rewarding than time and in any case ten is larger than nine. There was some very bitter feuding over this church, because it was built by a fop who had the gall to change the ground plan against all the regulations. We knew this builder and we can tell you that we liked him, however much he may have been something of a libertine."

"What's that you say?" interposed the elderly man, "This church is out of order and contravenes the rules of good architecture? And to think that it took me till today to recognise it!"

"You are quite correct in your observations," remarked the lady, "however, would you guess that this hat of mine has seen nine seasons of service as a hothead of idiosyncrasy? Yes, my dear, both the basilica and my hat are part of the furniture here and their transgressions have become part of the world order. Because, let me say it again, time lends dignity even to monstrosities."

Hear! Hear! Aren't these conversations worth coming back to? Are they a disturbance to those who trudge towards labour? Do they want for honesty? Do they not reek of what is nearly the ultimate mediocrity?

THE SPA TOWN OF LITTLE KARLSBAD

On the remarkable River Orsh there lies a town of good reputation and good water. The water bubbles up in shady places and the nine most powerful springs, secured in nine wells, have been designated with the names of the nine Muses. This is the spa town of Little Karlsbad. It is a town open to view, built half in brick and half in mud and stone, a town of doubtful construction and enduring health.

"There are no loafers here, mind you," the mayor of the spa is used to saying as he cuts a deck of cards. "Tally ho! Ours is a community forever on the go, running the race and arriving at the sixth month of June without delay and duly awaiting the regular deadline."

Well then, in this distant realm of purposeful activity, where there is no time to lose (alas, see how age bears down upon its citizens while it gives an air of legality to their assets), there were several smallholdings and some fairly ancient properties. They were acquired for the most part thanks to a card game variously known as Little and Large and Tiny Takes All. These assets were blessed and well administered, because, as God is my witness, the local burghers are thoroughly versed in their trades and are not deterred by the fact that, as spas go, Little Karlsbad is in the ninth band where size is concerned. Nor are they deterred by the unseasonable cloud cover and the feeble efforts of the sun to break through it, by the impermeability of the soil or by the thermal inadequacies of its hot springs. Let it be so! They may lack a public sewage system here, but this is a good-natured and respectable town.

TIME

The Gregorian calendar turned red for the first Sunday of June and the great bells pealed. Time moved forward at a rapid pace, as it always did at times of leisure or on great feast-days. Eight o'clock was approaching, the time whose snout, where the hours are concerned, is always said to be at the head of the pack, the time which will always track you down, whatever the cost.

THE AGE AND LOCATION
OF ANTONY HUSSEY'S ESTABLISHMENT

This is the moment when, with a song and a game of whimsy, the curtain opens on a tale set in the floating domicile of the Hussey family. Various light structures serving the swimming trade have been built onto Antony's raft-like erection, which has been tied at a point where the poppling Orsh has ripples along its back, sniffing at a sandbank that runs for as much as a hundred yards. In this area the bank on the town side of the river is covered in willows, which reach as far as the gardens of the leather dressers and wafer producers. Each year the willows get out of hand, preserving an unmanicured appearance that almost exceeds the bounds of decency. No one trims them and for those who make their way to the river there is nothing but a smattering of footpaths which are, alas, narrow. At the beginning of each pathway an inscription has been fixed to an indifferently painted pole, which carries its message rather as a female donkey carries her saddle. The announcement reads: River Resort.

"Why yes," said the burgrave, when sometime back in the fourteenth century he determined for once to speak in a straightforward manner, "Why yes, let us take the waters!" With these words he set off through the undergrowth to the sandbank, where his words became deeds. Since those times, for as long as anyone can remember, the area has been consecrated to the same purpose.

ANTONY HUSSEY

Having finished his song, Antony the Great clasped his hands behind his back and started breathing stealthily onto the ball of the thermometer. The column was virtually implacable in the face of such bribery and barely moved. Making a mental note of its probity, Mr Hussey found several thoughts taking turns to run through his head, like a sequence of shuffled cards.

Words finally broke his silence as he turned his back on the apparatus of Anders Celsius. "Such a summer, seems to me, spells misfortune. It is cold and I have ice on my breath, no matter that I haven't been taking draughts of water. What month is left to us, in which we might take care of our health and purify our bodies, when even June proves unpropitious for this purpose?

Very well, then. Be the climate propitious or not, such things brook no delay."

With these words the master lifeguard proceeded to undo his belt, remove his clothes and look down at the water in which his long hairy legs, the edge of the pool and the heavenly firmament were mirrored. He noticed the reflection of an upturned glass, which someone or other had placed crudely right on the edge, and added:

"Ah well. A swimming-pool empty of people and a cup empty of drink."

OF MATTERS CONTEMPORARY AND A PRIEST

At this moment Canon Gruntley, who held the moral life in higher esteem than any other man, appeared on the embankment bordering the other side of the river. While he was reciting some poem or prayer appropriate to the hour of day, time granted him the opportunity to peek in all directions. In this particular location it was not difficult to set eyes upon the master of bathing ceremonies, Antony Hussey, his tongue protruding from his lips and his moist eyes fastened upon a small glass.

"I say," exclaimed the canon, "I do declare, my dear sir, you're making a late start to the sabbath! Did the bells ring too softly for your ears? Detach yourself from that broomstick between your thighs which is plain for all to see. Part company with all that is abominable before it proves to be your ruin. Procure some coat or cloth from the rail beside this vile sewer. Otherwise, by George, I shall move to the other side and empty your bottle into the Orsh."

"So be it," responded Antony, shifting position, "Do as you wish and come across. Hurry over and see for yourself the particulars of your error. Search high and low in every corner for a broom, and if your skills extend so far as to find my bottle anything but empty, I will not hold it against you.

Get going, strike out across the stream in your sandals. I would like to acquaint you with some home truths which must be heard before it's too late."

The priest closed his book, keeping a forefinger clamped between the pages, took a pew on the stone edge of the stream and began a reply at once scolding and susceptible to the constraints of a civil conversation.

"What sort of vermin," he began, "discards its trousers as easily as an honourable man removes his hat? Who mentored such manners? Who inculcated such a code of behaviour in your head?"

"Very well," came the reply from Antony, lighting a cigar he'd unexpectedly come upon in the pocket of a coat which some customer had forgotten the previous day, "All right, I can tell you something about my teachers, who were without exception good souls and erudite scholars. However, do not mistake me for a man given to indecency. I removed my underclothes for a good reason. You must understand that the human skin, as has been made clear to this day in the schools I attended for my early education, is adapted to breathing and demands satisfaction in this respect. These principles were instilled into me, while I in turn accepted them and have always observed them to the great benefit of my body. I have had enough of your book of odes, enough of seeing that finger of yours chewing over one and the same worn-out line of which it fails to make anything like sense. Be off with you, expositor of unwholesomeness, bound by gibbering letters and panting lines which wend their whimsied way in accordance with rules."

Having delivered himself of these words, the manager of the lido began a slow descent of the steps before collapsing into the pool.

"You see me here," he continued, bearing up manfully in the cold water, "as one prepared to make riposte to all those calumnies which you have heaped upon me since I was five. However, my hands are wet. It is too late to remove the cigar from my mouth and yet too soon to throw it away."

"Heavens above," exclaimed the holy man, "do you wish to re-enact the fable of the crow who lost the cheese! For the love of God hold your cigar and your tongue too."

PRIVATE HUGO

During such exchanges, fine-tuned in their fierceness, a man of about fifty appeared at Hussey's lido. He had the calves of a fencer 'en garde' and hands firmly planted inside gloves. He was accoutred like an English master of the hunt and his unscarred royalist face bore a fatty cyst the size of a nut above the line of his left jaw.

"Good day to you," he began from behind a cloud of choice fragrances known to any stable.

"Good day to you too," came the rejoinder from Master Hussey, "I'm doing my swimming exercise. You will be at home with this drill, while to the canon it is sufficient grounds for a fit of apoplexy. Pray indulge me in a final circuit of my little reservoir."

"No question about it. Provided the padre does not take offence, I'd prefer not to stand in your way," were the words which proceeded from the new arrival as he billeted himself on a stool, while Master Hussey, cigar in mouth, ruffled the surface of the pool.

The man of God on the far bank laid down his book, marking the page, and reciprocated the greeting.

"Good morning, Major. Do you think that you have been making the right choice in showing indulgence towards a foolish man whose mind lacks a single mark of distinction?"

"Certainly," came the hunter's reply, "The master's physical training has put him in good shape and his mind, even though he's no more than a lifeguard, is nimble enough to run rings around you with its replies. I could have stopped him entering the water, but by the time I arrived he'd taken the plunge and was already afloat. Why should I disturb something in full flood?"

"Stuff and nonsense!" exclaimed the priest, "You were always a stickler for timing, though you'd clear- ly pass by a timeless truth without a glance. Well so be it, you will be made to answer for these errors. The book which I have just laid down is at hand to remind us of things eternal. It is two thousand years old. Major, take heed of what I want to say to you."

"Sir," Hussey intervened as he emerged from the depths, "the major has not read your book and is not going to read it, indeed would not read it were it even more antique than it already is. Could he be so foolish as to believe that old donkeys have a better bray? This jaeger is after fish and you, shouting at the top of your lungs, are driving them away."

Meanwhile the major opened a box which he'd brought with him from Hussey's storeroom, attached an earthworm to a fishhook and cast the line into the stream.

"On the contrary," he averred, "I detect some note of enthusiasm in these speeches. Even when they happen to lack nobility, I tolerate them because enthusiasm is a reflection of passion. Where can we find greatness but in a sky eternally blue and passions eternally bloody?"

OBSERVATIONS ON CLIMATE

"Perhaps the canon will supply you with an answer, if you wish to know it," remarked the master lifeguard as he dived into a shirt. "However, I do not believe that you will be able to maintain your point concerning a blue sky. All in all, you see, this June has been a washout. I know that you wanted to juxtapose an azure blue with blood, but such an endeavour is excessive, however blue-blooded you may be yourself. Think carefully, Major. Does it not occur to you that the weather is damnably inclement and the rain barely holds off? I see a mass of clouds with only fissures of blue, and even that hardly seems real.

Look around at the heavens from all four points of the compass," Antony went on, his face hidden in his shirt and his sleeve describing a huge circle in the air with his arm stuck halfway inside it. "Look around and you will see nothing but traversal layers of risen mist. See how the currents rise, see the vapour drawn off the surface of the earth until it reaches the dewpoint. See all those layers and banks of cloud in the shape of intrigue. Alas, Gentlemen, anger is not permitted me, such is the impecuniousness of my condition. Nevertheless, I should like an almost immediate licence to swear."

FURTHER DISCUSSIONS

"Whence comes this embarrassment?" exclaimed the canon, "have I not been treated to a whole hour of your expletives?"

Antony replied that the priest could be mistaken, because during a season like this the distance to the other bank of the Orsh was considerable.

"Your ears," he pointed out, "were ringing from the droning of your books, which are raucous even when shut. While I merely gave out two or three sighs, you must have been hearing one of your Church Fathers."

He followed up these words by putting on his trousers without a hitch and having buttoned them up sat down beside the major. The royalist, whose patience was not inexhaustible, jerked the rod and having removed the hook tidied up the fishing gear. Then he stood up and calmly uncorked a bottle.

"If shouting were not your way of settling a quarrel," he commented as he filled three beakers, "I could be helpful to you now and again. However, so far as I can judge, you are only satisfied with having the last word."

A SLUR ON DUELS

This provoked a reply from Antony Hussey: "It is better to have the last word than to suffer the final blow. You can't convince me that it would cool my temper to have someone slice through my calf to the shinbone. The medical books which I consult fail to appreciate anything that isn't a chronic illness. So far as they are concerned, to be quartered in a place where a point of honour is being settled is a gross scientific error. I say each to his own, Major. You owe it to this advanced century to die of your bedsores, overtaken by curvature of the spine as you reach your ninetieth year."

A COMPLICATION

Antony followed these words by taking a swig from his glass, and at just that moment his wife Kate arrived at the lido, steam rising from the saucepan she was carrying.

"Ah, you're never one to loaf about," she said to Antony without a smile.

"We are conversing about those abstract matters which preoccupy the canon," retorted the master, and going up to his wife he lifted the lid of the pan a little in order to discover whether good food lay within. Then he returned the lid to its former position and eyeing both the pan and the face of his consort offered the comment:

"Your kings, your canon's tomes and my health. How can I value them, Major, when things are like this."

"My husband prattles enough and more," said Mrs Hussey. "Oh! I have endured him since my seventeenth year. You see, I married young. No doubt about it, I could have chosen from better fellows than this bathing superintendent, but Antony gave the other potential bridegrooms a beating and having got his hands on some keys, which as luck would have it fitted my door, he pestered me for so long that a wedding ceremony became a necessity. It's all too true that Antony used to be very much in love and a picture of robust health into the bargain. I'd like to wager that those fellows received more than they could take when he gave them a thrashing."

A THOROUGH AND COMPREHENSIVE ANALYSIS (FOLLOWING THE ADVICE OF THE CRITICS)

The canon, for whom the scene with the saucepan recalled an engraving on the reverse side of a coin described by Beger in his Observationes et coniecturae in numismata quaedam antiqua, fell silent and in pensive mood flung stone after stone into the flowing Orsh.

"Such liveliness of conduct, such exaggerated playfulness," remarked Antony as he leant over towards the major "does not become a priest and the canon should abandon it. I have seen a sufficient number of confused souls who did as he does and ended up regretting their previous enthusiasm. A man who starts throwing weights about – light or heavy, it makes no difference – without proper training will act in such an inappropriate manner that the brain will dislodge the cerebellum and damage his brain stem."

It is said that several historians used to exercise their bodies," Antony continued, raising his voice, "and I used to hear there were a few runners among the admirers of literature. But is that a reason for the canon to go chasing through fields and hurdling over briars?"

"What would the magister thermarum be wanting to say?" asked the canon. "It seems to me that in the course of your journey towards articulation you have reached a level of incomprehensibility that is almost interesting."

RESOLVE AND ACTION

"I gather there's a barney between you about some nonsense," Mrs Hussey interposed, "and that you're yelling at each other as if money matters were at stake.

What a loudmouth that husband of mine is.

Often enough I used to say to him that in the summer months there should be a quietness and refinement about his words, because our living requires us to give a welcome to each and every customer, even the dirty devil who steals the soap and tears one of my towels into footrags in the changing room."

With these words the lady stepped into the boat and when she had cast off headed for the other bank of the Orsh and the man of God.

"My husband has no match," she explained, "when it comes to behaving like an ass. Come here, dear sir. I will be your ferryman and then you will be able to deliver your words of wisdom from close range."

OF BOTTLES AND BATTLES

Arriving at the bathing area, the canon greeted the major and seated himself beside him.

"Your glass has been too long full," remarked Hugo. "Would it not be better to give up on it?"

"You want me to pour away wine?" retorted the canon, "To pour away wine and to damage books are wrongs of the first order, sir!"

"Where wine is concerned I'm with you," agreed Antony, "I know a story about an innkeeper who was condemned to a dark cell for smashing the spigot on a competitor's cask of wine."

"Reminds me of the Italian campaign. Do you happen to know why the first battle of the Piave was lost?" asked Hugo, excited by the horrors of war.

Having realised that neither of his two friends wanted to hear any explanation from him, he began to talk about military positions and the wine cellars of Upper Italy anyway.

"You'll be aware," he said, turning to face Mrs Hussey, "you'll all be aware that there was a shortage of containers in the army and that they had to take their wine from a cupped hand. No avoiding the fact that soldiers had to pierce the barrels with their bayonets. A lovely stab in the lower regions and out trickled the stream of life. As a result the cellars were awash with wine and quite a few regiments drowned in the stuff. Opening a barrel with a bayonet is not an economical method and many drinks were spilt that way. Drinks which are just the ticket for rekindling the flame of courage when it's flickering and about to go out."

"Courage!" expostulated Antony, "The bleating courage of loudmouths that fire upon an enemy from some hideout. If you are a man of courage, pray lift a hundred kilos, Major, but do so quietly."

"Bunkum!" shouted the priest. "I can recite some verses which deal neither with scenes of carnage nor with weight-lifting, and yet they have conquered the world."

This was the moment for Babel around the bottle as each interrupted the others.

"Don't serve up any more of this whistling in the wind from libraries!" "See reason!" "Be silent!" "All this is the mischief that comes out of military headquarters and those people who hold up their chins with bandages."

A REPRIMAND

"I want to make it quite clear," said Hugo, "that a spot of peace and quiet is the only thing I could appreciate in people whose professions lack value. However, you keep yelling your head off! Pipe down! I will take up the challenge with this weapon and then you'll know my answer to you."

The major followed up these words by grabbing hold of a rod used to straighten the limbs of those learning to swim, and from a squatting position he proceeded to take a powerful swipe at the empty bottle.

"Heavens above!" exclaimed Antony, "what do you think you're doing? Can't you see that the padre is about to shock himself into an early grave?"

However, the canon was merely leafing through the pages of his book. Having found the passage he was looking for, he spoke as follows:

"All right, so be it, take a fist or a club to this hideout of pornography and scatter it to the four winds. Its fate is richly deserved. Use every ounce of strength. I know just how to take you down a peg or two."

Then he approached the major, whose displays of ferocious hostility showed no signs of abating and, declaiming in a haughty voice, quoted from Book VII of the Odes of Horace. Antony the Great, ignorant of any other means by which the strength that erupts and bursts forth from a healthy body might be harnessed, grabbed hold of a block of wood and lifted it above his head a hundred and one times.

COURTSHIP

Listening to the canon while he showered upon them a multitude of beautiful verses, Mrs Catherine Hussey crossed her hands and clasped them to her bosom as she delivered the following:

"Here I am, sir, and I'm listening to what you're saying. They claim that Latin is the language of the Romans, but I've been told it's a tongue that failed to survive and is now deceased. You have shown us that this is stuff and nonsense, for you have spoken it so skilfully and for long enough to let us see the error of such claims.

However, now you have the chance to relax and tell me something in our mother tongue, because I must confess that I am only halfway towards understanding speeches in Latin. They are so copious! It seems to me that these well-organised expressions are a little over-articulated, coming across as they do like a shower of hailstones, but I have no doubt that you are giving utterance to worthy sentiments.

Oh dear me, no doubt about it. There were those good old times when we made time fly with our teasing tales of whimsy, with singing and playing musical instruments. Oh sir, if you had heard a certain organ builder who used to pinch me in the side as he crooned one song after another, you would have become like a man possessed. I am convinced that his creativeness is in many respects on a par with your skill in handicrafts, albeit you've seen many a foreign country and attended schools until well advanced in years."

After this speech the lady proceeded to sweep hooks, lines and other necessary components of the fisherman's art off the bench, before stepping across the washboard, which had fallen onto the ground, and then dragging the bench to the southern end of the bathing arena.

"Well now, my dear sir," Catherine Hussey continued once she had sat down on the bench, "Come here, come beside me, this seat is not as uncomfortable as you seem to think. We can manage without Latin here.

These two," she added, pointing towards the master lifeguard and the major, "will fail to understand a single word of it. I'd wager that they are entertaining each other with tales of firearms and lunatic sports competitions. Look at my husband there, flexing the muscles in his left arm. Doubtless he wants to persuade the major that he is a tower of strength. What am I supposed to do with an overbearing man who is always shouting only because he values breathing exercises and thinks they're giving him a bigger chest? I look at the way he hops and jumps through every day; what can I do with a man trying to pole vault up to the ceiling?"

"It may be the case" came the reply from the canon, "that the master of the lido cares for his body a tad too much, but I never egged him on or gave him any encouragement to act in such an unrestrained manner. The master, you and I, madam, are all of an age when we no longer have the lungpower for a full-throated roar and when we somehow find the ability to pass by our neighbour's fence without trying to leap over it. As for myself, I am not given to ostentatious tricks."

THE PATH OF VIRTUE

"Just so, just so, reverend sir," Mrs Hussey agreed as she rose from her seat, "on the other hand, taking into account your own age you should show a little more forbearance. As you can see, my husband indulges in some innocent game. It is perhaps foolish, but it is not depraved and does not deserve such harsh condemnation. I do not know what rancour has taken hold of you, or what has made you sound the alarm in this way. For God's sake! And then you go back to your Latin, which turns out to be such irritating nonsense."

Catherine followed up these words by turning to her husband and telling him that the canon was a deviant and a man to beware of.

"Oh," began the rejoinder from Antony Hussey, "such things leave me cold. They simply don't concern me."

And leaving the woman bereft of any fuller explanation, he encouraged the major to demonstrate some military manoeuvre he was speaking about.

"Like this, Like this," exclaimed Hugo, selecting a gap between planks in the paling to receive a stabbing from the rod. For it bore some distant resemblance to the space between someone's ribs.

COURTING ANEW

"What a sinister creature you are, Major" opined Mrs Hussey. "Forever covered in sweat, legs forever astride, arm outstretched and flashes of lightning in your eyes. You almost remind me of a sergeant with whom I was on terms of some familiarity in my younger days. Ah, what a man about town he was. There's so much to be said about him. He was cantankerous just like you are and I often had to pacify him when he flew off the handle all of a sudden. I offered him anything that I considered appropriate in order to tame that temper of his. But his fingers went on tearing at buttons with too much impatience and he went on drinking bottle after bottle. He served in the auxiliary supply corps while you went into the artillery regiment, so you never saw red trousers."

"I never wore them and it was just as well for me," pointed out the major, "seeing that those regiments were full of village oafs."

"Is that so?" asked the lady, "I've never heard anyone say that before. In our street the men in red trousers sold like hot cakes.

You will be aware of the fact, sir, that I am a townswoman, and that I came to this godforsaken place only against my better judgment. I get goose pimples just thinking of our latest guests. The infantry, where weapons and uniforms are concerned, are a far cry from the cavalry, but a hundred, a thousand times better than the inhabitants of this place. Among the crowd of sickly fellows who hurry here every summer a smart corporal from the 28th would be something remarkable. And I would be lost then.

In my day the canon was already old, but do explain by what stroke of ill luck I was prevented from ever meeting you."

"But, but, but…" came from the major as he lapsed into a moderate state of fury, "…perhaps some unseasoned novice turned up at my howitzers, one of those chaps who could arouse the female cooks with his gosling beard and whom I used to torment.

Do not reproach me for these things. The choice made by the women had nothing to do with any plans of mine. Incidentally, so far as I know your husband, to whom you are obliged to show all respect because he recruited you from an abominable part of town, served neither in auxiliary supply nor as an artillery man but was digging trenches."

"How could I not know that! As if I didn't realise where he did his service," replied the lady. "If you want to start an argument say that again and Master Antony will have your guts for garters, despite this club of yours which you seem to suppose is a rapier. I can assure you that my Antony will not suffer anyone to speak to his wife in a frivolous manner."

THE AMIABLE SWIMMING INSTRUCTOR
Meanwhile nine o'clock on this Sunday morning approached and the pool was graced by several ladies who, come rain or shine, subordinated themselves to the demands of a good bodily condition. Antony greeted them in the most ostentatious manner.

"Pray come in," he ventured, "Do not hesitate to join us. You must not permit yourselves to be disturbed by any feeling of inclemency. The canon and the major have intimated to me that the waters are in a warmish condition."

"Good day to you," saluted Hugo, touching his hat.

"Good day" came their reply, the major's rakish reputation drawing languorous smiles out of them.

"Make your way towards the places assigned to you," the instructor continued, "here is a tunic which you will find to be an item of necessity, a towel and some soap. If you need any further attention, be so good as to call out three times so that I can be with you as soon as it's appropriate."

"My husband may be addle-pated," interposed Mrs Hussey, "but that's not to say he doesn't know what his rights are or how to cut up rough in getting his entitlement."

"If he had made a rough cut of his rights, if he had severed them at a slice, incinerated or immersed them, in a word liberated himself from them, he would have earned the title Master, but this way he is only Antony."

"Obviously," began a further retort from the woman, "I know he's Antony, because my name's Catherine."

"Splendid," cried the man of God, "I see that you have acquainted yourself with a smattering of logic. My defences are therefore down."

A CAUTIONARY TALE

Meanwhile the women made their appearance unattired and shrieked as they entered water which bore down on their haunches like a cane.

"In company like this," began Antony, while he attempted to seat himself on the canon's tome, "the discussion will make considerable progress. I am sure that the canon will forget his Ovidian Metamorphoses while gazing at those of the fair sex who have been thirty for some years now. In fact, Major, your own age represents the most perfect example of a refusal to metamorphose."

"I'm leaving," responded the major, "because as a rule there's always one of these highly-skilled lady bathers who will aspire to start drowning right in front of us. Be resolute in cases of necessity and be careful where the girl in trouble is underage."

The canon objected that they needn't take any notice of anyone, but this didn't stop Hugo from packing up his boxes and giving no further thought to fishing.

"Major," said Antony, "Never have I behaved towards you in a callous manner, but I am afraid that I am now compelled to use force in order to keep you here. It is essential for this health resort, this ill-fated raft, to be alive with people, at least on the outside. It is so helpful to have you appear, full-figured and fifty, provided that you remain sitting here. I can overlook the rod and your pursuit of the fish in my own backyard, but I cannot tolerate you on the far bank. You surely wouldn't want these women to climb out of the water and for my pool to remain empty for the rest of the day. Surely you wouldn't like to be the cause of my business going to the wall."

"It seems to me," opined the major with a gesture of disapproval, "that you are identifying us with those bar flies who prop up the pub trade. And another leaf from my book says that you take our tolerance too much for granted."

"Tolerance," the master lifeguard came back at him, "top and bottom of military leadership."

ERNESTO THE MAGICIAN

During these discussions Ernesto the magician, newly arrived in Little Karlsbad, passed by the famous willows. Aware of being worn out and unclean after a long journey, he spotted a cosy enough spot for a dip and after a moment's hesitation climbed down onto the footpath, made his way across the narrowest of planks and unexpectedly found himself in the bathing area.

"I see that it's brightening up and noon will see it hot," said Antony, "so you may strip for action, gentlemen. Not you, however, the one who's just turned up, you should wait a minute to cool down because you're dripping with sweat."

"Touched me on a tender spot you have, sir, oh yes," remonstrated Ernesto. "Do you know that for a whole week I've had nothing but a candle to keep me warm? I am Ernesto the magician and where this harsh climate is concerned (for I hail from Southern climes) there are several points on the surface of my body which every evening play host to the flame."

"Oh," exclaimed Mrs Hussey, "is it really you, the one who's been the talk of the whole town since yesterday? Yes, it's you! My sources tell me, sir, that you are a fire-eater, used to stay in Paris and have come here from the Low Countries."

"I've been all over the place," replied the magician with a touch of uncertainty, "but if there's a lot of talk about someone, it probably isn't about me! I turned up at nine o'clock with our waggon. We have established ourselves in the square. From there, having spent a few moments in the office of a gentleman who acts as police constable, I came to this riverside resort. However, if there is some swindler here passing himself off as a magician, then I will have no alternative but to leave, without arranging any performance and without taking the waters."

"There's no need for impatience," responded the lady. "Who's been saying such things? You are with us now and this is where you will be staying.

These men," she added, making available large and small brushes for the ladies, who had requested them for their complexions, "are so touchy. No sooner have I said to the magician that he's a magician than he starts an argument over whether he might not be the magician."

"One magician is very much like another," said the women who were busy at work with the brushes. "There's always some shaggy-maned performer with an audience for his glass-munching and the nine wigs he plucks from his sleeve."

"I don't know about that," responded Mrs Hussey, "but unlike the locals here Mr Ernesto has his own head of curls and doesn't look like a man in thrall to weaponry or scholarship."

THE MAGICIAN'S APPEARANCE
In the meantime Ernesto undid his coat and started undressing, placing his clothing item by item on a nail and on the latch. At last he emerged, uncovering a narrow back and a rib cage which stuck out at the rear by several inches. His beautiful Flemish leotard made a swimsuit redundant.

"It might be attire meant for other occasions," commented the major, "but why should we not permit it here?"

"There is something indecent about it," declared the canon. "It is in your interests, Antony, to make your guest put his trousers on. Do you not realise that all a man's extremities may stick out in a garment like this, and are you not able to observe that the leotard is pink? Pink is the colour of piglets."

Antony was clearing away the remains of the food, bearing off a broad wooden tray loaded with stacked saucepans and plates, but when he heard the remarks of the canon he turned round, clutching the load, ready to contradict him.

"There we have it," he remarked by way of closing the conversation, "If pink is the colour of piglets, then a scholarly grey and black is the colour of sewer-rats."

INARTICULATE PROFESSORS

"Gadzooks!" expostulated the major. "Pool Captain, you absolutely never give in, do you. How did you come by that silver tongue of yours?"

"In all manner of ways," he replied. "Let me tell you the one that matters most: I was never a bookworm.

Five or six years back there was a professor from the Charles University living here. The man was circumspect by nature but a streetfighter with the written word. He shook up the literary world, classical and contemporary. And you know what, he couldn't manage a coherent statement identifying the number of the cabin where he'd disrobed. From that moment on I have taken the view that such erudition is a hindrance when we wish to express an opinion."

COMELINESS DOES NOT BECOME A GENIUS

Ernesto the magician took no part in these discussions. He stood with his legs crossed, leaning against the handrail of the pool, observing the scene and enjoying a smoke. In a nutshell, he stood there watching and standing there he watched.

"I observe," said the major, "that a crooked chest does nothing to dent the ego of magicians."

"I am not clear how things stand with magicians, but it is certainly the case that Byron walked with a limp. It is also a fact that Homer was blind, Socrates was of bestial appearance and district inspectors stammer," said the canon.

"There's a remarkable arbitrariness in all that," Antony added. "Is it not possible to determine the type once and for all?"

A DISCUSSION BETWEEN THE MAGICIAN
AND MRS HUSSEY

In the meantime Catherine, who was no longer needed in the women's section, arrived with a bucket in tow full of dirty water. When she'd poured the contents away she proceeded to converse.

"There is scarcely anything to marvel at in a summer like this. Yesterday it rained and if I'm not mistaken it will rain just as much today. Tell me, sir, is the weather as abysmal as this in the Low Countries?"

"A mite better," Ernesto replied, "although on Sunday it tends to rain just the same as here. The rain sets in around ten o'clock and continues till noon. It clears up after that and all the inhabitants rush off to the performance, because in those far-flung corners of the earth there is a hunger for enlightenment among the people."

"Well now," the lady replied, putting down the bucket, "is this a principle that admits of no exception? Are there not bathing superintendents in those Netherlands who would exploit their business opportunities as much as possible precisely when the weather is clearing up? Is it really allowable, is it really acceptable, in view of the losses which would flow from such an action, to abandon the pool? My husband wouldn't do it. Not my husband, not even if there was a drum roll to usher in the Last Judgment. My husband is insatiable!"

The magician expressed the view that this was inexcusable, and the lady nodded in agreement.

"Just so! Just so! I never stop telling him day in and day out. But do you by any chance know what is responsible for his condition?

He has passed his half century without leaving Little Karlsbad. He is almost fluent in his reading and writing, but physical exercise is his particular forte, because not even nightfall, when sleep beckons, will curb his gymnastics."

"Therein lies the stumbling block," opined Ernesto. "I would be prepared to wager that his exercise has a soulless quality, that he is doing himself harm in order to feed an unhealthy passion, and that he acts simply in order to serve his money grubbing ways."

A SMALL EXAMPLE OF ERNESTO'S ARTISTRY

His point concluded, Ernesto approached the major, who had taken out his stopwatch.

"See here," he said, his eyes fixed upon the timepiece, "I am engaged in exercises myself. However much they call into play the body, to a large extent they are exercises of the mind. Now look, I will make this object vanish, without your noticing where it's disappeared to or how it went. It will involve the merest touch, a touch triggered by long deliberation and much mental exercise."

At this moment the magician sneezed and the men took half a step backwards.

"Now then," he continued, his eyes fixed on an empty palm, "could you tell me, sir, what the time is?"

And before an oath could leave Hugo's lips or a lengthier form of words depart from the canon, Ernesto pulled the stopwatch out of his mouth between bulging cheeks.

"Brrr!" he added, drying the instrument with his elbow, "My crown feels frozen between the two hemispheres of my brain and I hear a sound not unlike the tolling of Easter bells, for this timepiece of glass and metal has caused a cooling of my cranial core and has incited it to mutiny with its ticking."

BOUNDLESS ADMIRATION

"Good heavens," exclaimed Mrs Hussey, her wonder knowing no limits. "Did you really have the watch inside your head? That ticker belonging to a bloodthirsty man?"

THE MAJOR EXPRESSES AN OPINION

"You're a man of talent and deserve some recompense," said Hugo. Then he added, noting an awkward movement on the part of Ernesto and a look of displeasure from the canon: "This is my opinion, one you may not share but you cannot change.

So far as this morning is concerned," he remarked as he turned once again to face Ernesto, "we can merely offer you something smoked, by which I mean five sausages and a tot of rum."

"You said something about sausages," came the response from Mrs Hussey as she made a beeline from pantry to pool, "and offered to bear the cost. Here they are."

The magician was quick to indicate that he was used to such food and much appreciated it. Then straddling the bench he wolfed down three pairs of sausages very quickly and without the least embarrassment. Finally, when he had wiped his mouth, he drank up the rum.

FOREIGN LAND, FULL OF HATRED

"Oh my, oh my, oh my," he volunteered, flicking away a morsel of onion, "I didn't think that in these remote regions I would find men so forward-thinking. When it comes to appreciation my audiences show restraint. Sometimes they shower me with things which are far from edible.

In Mülhausen and Schenewiden they almost gave me a hiding. There was a hue and cry about my having appropriated the Lady Mayor's ring, which was nowhere to be found. Nonetheless it was not of my doing. It became untraceable, like so many other items of public property."

"Come on now," said Mrs Hussey, "What really happened?"

Came the reply:

"It was like this: Schenewiden is a town in the region of Austria known as Steiermark. People there forever have a tune on their lips and a smug grin on their faces. I was standing in the square following the ancient custom of all travelling actors, carried away in preparing for my performance, when I came upon some ladies with their charges. I praised them for their trim necks, seeing that they had the goitre. Several quarrelsome fellows were airing views about the weather. I was minding my own business, steering clear of a scrap."

"I have no doubt that you're not a man to go brawling," suggested Mrs Hussey, "but what happened with the ring?"

"With the ring?" He returned to the point. "Oh, I took that without any trouble. Light fingers, no vulgar display. I threw it into thin air and that's where it vanished. Those Steiermarkians, dregs of humanity, incurably suspicious, wouldn't think the archbishop had his official residence in the area, frisked me for all of two hours. They set up some policeman to follow my every movement. I was lucky to give him the slip in the nick of time. There was nothing left of said constable but the plume of his helmet in the distance."

"Oh of course, people are uncouth" said Catherine, and pointing a finger at her sensitive breast and simple-minded head she added:

"Leave them. Leave them to choke on their own folly. You said there was an archbishop in the area – just let them try behaving discourteously in front of him! He'll chastise them in the end! They'll find there's no escaping their comeuppance!"

"Retribution follows one step behind the offence," said the major. "Even so, I would like my watch back. I'd hate to have to be uncouth like those chappies from Mülhausen."

Ernesto had two or three disarming remarks, the sort that trip forth easily, on the tip of his tongue. In this instance, however, seeing that there was nothing else to be done, he retrieved the item from his deepest pocket.

THE PASSAGE OF TIME

"The hours fly by," he said, "and it is not in my power to hold them back.

Come on, it's almost noon and the tools of my trade are still hitched to the waggon."

Having proffered these words Ernesto pulled on his trousers, draped a coat over his Flemish leotard, which was still dry, and threw himself into drumming up an audience before bidding farewell with a polite bow.

The priest and the major followed in his wake.

PEACE BREAKS OUT

"I say," said Mrs Hussey, while the magician was walking through the willows on the path into town, buttoning up his clothes as he went, "Look what we have here. Buffoonery with a stick, leaping into water, deep breathing exercises, the canon with his bookish gobbledygook, the major with his horseplay, all chips off the same useless block. Ernesto is a dashing fellow! Just where could any of you acquire such charm?

Did you notice, Antony, his look of embarrassment and the way he blushed when the major offered him food in such an overbearing way?"

The maestro took the bottle and without replying held it against the sky. "Yes," he commented, after a moment's careful consideration, "he's a man who knows what he's doing. He ate, he drank his fill and he avoided the entrance fee."

TWILIGHT IDYLL

In the environs of Little Karlsbad night announces itself through the usual process of darkening, just as happens at those ends of the earth represented by faraway Prague. To places accustomed to shade, gorges and ravines comes the darkness, while at the same time the local mayor, (if the town clock is not ahead of itself), walks in the open spaces of the square, oblivious to the graceful arrival of the evening.

According to the season of the year, in its own time, the darkness of night swoops down from the treetops, where it has been roosting since the previous day. Pockets of cold spread themselves out and black-winged space forces its way inside the container that is Little Karlsbad.

Prudent people seal their lips and break no silence before they have taken food. It is night and the mayor notes that evening has begun. It arrives just as he says it will and his words are proved right. Night has fallen. In front of their houses skinny maidens settle and search the heavens for the evening star. 'Omnia sumus sine sole', they latinise. Into darkness are we plunged.

But praise the Lord, for there are goodly, hospitable establishments everywhere, whose doors venture out in a half-yawn during the day but in the evening are wide open and well lighted.

MENUISING

Mr Hussey, the major and the canon arrived at that ancient place of refreshment The Fourteen Helpers, where they made merry.

"Let's tuck in to the food and drink," said Hugo. "Bring me some dinner. Cheese full of fat, venison, poultry, lamb, anything born alive or hatched from an egg. Bring me anything I can eat that ripens, anything finned or skinned, bring me all those gastropods consumed in civilised countries. Fetch them here! It is evening, the earth has done its rounds and that is when custom dictates that we eat."

"Would you say, Major" proffered the canon, "that you have become a glutton or a windbag? Do you wish to treat us to a display of your teeth or your tongue?"

"If I knew my way around words, I would hold my tongue, just as you do, Padre," retorted Hugo. "Right then. I'm not ordering you to take up your weapons, but start attacking the food!"

The canon made the point that he felt indisposed when too much was being said and Antony remarked, while applying a ladle to the soup:

"Indisposed? But the dinner has barely begun.

This," he added, turning his handlebar moustache to the man of God, "is the product of a faulty diet. You are sicklied o'er with the pale cast of thought! You even give in to meditation at dinnertime, which is a way of taking gluttony beyond all bounds."

"Then forgive me," said the priest. "Why should we quarrel afresh?"

"Because," came the reply from the overseer of the baths, "because you are killing yourself. Because you are half a century in the tooth. Because you persevere in the faith of your bad habits.

If I'd been five minutes up to the ears in the water of my bathing pool, you'd have hauled me out with all your strength. Well then, may I not be permitted to warn you that you are drowning in an error far worse than water?"

"The ideas in that head of yours, Antony," vouchsafed the major, "are monstrous. Or does this bottle of wine remind you of the River Orsh?'

"No, no and no once more."

"Or yes and yes again."

"Wherever has the salt gone?"

"What about the vinegar?"

"Do you remember how in the olden days we salted our toast and spread dripping over it?"

"Those were the days!"

"Here they are, these Ciceronian tongues, tongues tied and – when we cut the frenulum – tongues loosened!"

The major, the canon and Antony tucked into their meal and washed it down with wine. Fin to begin, then dish of mutton, plate of spinach, leg of venison with cranberry smattering, asparagus, minor garnishing of salad, cake, sliver of stewed fruit, unstewed fruit (damn it, unripe too so far as the grapes are concerned) and cheese in nine kinds.

The reckoning!

"Bring the bill, waiter, and a fresh bottle of wine. But do not bestir yourself unduly from excess of zeal, because it needs to be carried with care."

"This way! Fine. Here's your money."

"Gentlemen, we can decamp," said the major, "because if my memory serves me right we're off to see that magician perform."

"Well, well," commented Antony, "Went out of my mind entirely, and wasn't anywhere in yours either, Padre. I'd lay odds that an expectant Ernesto is on the lookout for your hats and might even be missing the sight of my cap."

"If it was not in my mind," explained the canon, "that was merely in deference to you, because I discerned that you seemed to be more than happy to drink on."

"You put half a bottle inside yourself, and if you downed it without a taste for it so much the worse for you," retorted the major.

"So much the better, I'd say, so much the better for us. I dread to think how things might have turned out if the padre had been thirsty."

With these words, Antony cleaned his moustache with his sleeve and took hold of a bunch of flowers protruding from a vase in the middle of the table.

"Time for the off," said Hugo.

And off they went.

The square was an eighteenth century creation, to which a gruesome supplement generated by the products of some college of applied arts had been added. With its dark clusters of plane trees and gleaming street lights, embellished by a cupola which glowed like stars, it fell only slightly short of being beautiful.

SATAN'S ARMOURY

"If that devil of yours was standing right behind us, Padre," vouchsafed Antony, "he could impale any one of us on his pitchfork, because make no mistake about it, we take a fancy to the fair sex and are rushing headlong to see the magician's tricks.

See here, this rascal Ernesto must have been running round the whole town, blowing his own trumpet, because how else could he have attracted such a crowd?"

"I must ask you to explain yourself, Antony," replied the canon, "I do not have a devil and the devil has no pitchfork."

"By gad! You are a libertine," exclaimed the major, "Your perversion colours the way you look at everything. The pool captain is not mistaken. The devil keeps a firm grip on the handle of his pitchfork and Ernesto has indeed been scurrying about everywhere in town.

That's how it is," he added, just when the path of the three friends was being intercepted by some young lady, bringing out the old longing mixed with pain, "Goodness knows there are very few attractive girls round here, but some there are. Each has her own way of turning the screw, and if any of these rare specimens are in Little Karlsbad, they'll be out tonight."

Women were not a subject worth mentioning, but this did not prevent the master lifeguard and the major from referring to them at length and without pause.

"Look here," said Antony, observing a girl go hurrying past, "I would like to determine once and for all how the proportions of the calf are correlated with the age and overall dimensions of the body taken as a whole."

"Enough, put this mischief out of your mind and let's get a move on, the show has already started."

And so the three friends linked arms and kept in step while walking, as people used to do when a good military training applied:

By the left, quick march, left!

Antony was walking in the middle. A man tall enough to extinguish the street lights without a ladder, a man unmissable and proudly aware of his own size, garrulous, restless and penniless. Antony, for whom silence was not an imperative, began to air his opinions concerning magicians, taxing the patience of his friends and committing gross errors of judgment on the fundamentals of conjuring.

CONCERNING MAGICIANS

"No doubt the general public, men and women with stomachs full and livers lily, rails against these amazing magicians who walk in the wasteland and are to be found at any crossroads spinning their hats to choose direction. No doubt these people turn tail whenever there's someone to give chase. They don't look back and they wilt before the prospect of fisticuffs.

For has anyone seen them slapping the face of a local dignitary in a merry tumble? Or has anyone watched them dine from the well-stocked dishes at the Lord Mayor's table?

They make their escape through the woods, seeking adventure among groups of harvesters resting by a natural spring. Their getaway takes them through some deserted village, where walking or breaking into a run they perform a trick or two in front of the women who mount guard over their chickens during harvest-time, counting and re-counting them without pause. They are on the run until the day when their innocent capers culminate in an ingenious robbery, a scientific masterpiece, a rebel's mantle or a role in government.

Mark my words, Canon. Mark them well, Major. The magician who has grown wise finds gloves for his hands and a stiff and bulging hat for his head. Combed and domed, he may become whatever he chooses.

Your noble descent, Major, is the invention of some scatterbrained swindler, a man who received more of a beating than he deserved and more than an ordinary person could have endured. The progenitor of your line was a street magician who bettered himself by some convenient thieving and then found a legal method for multiplying his gains.

Alas, Major! You fall short of that ingenuity that could bring you to barony. I regret to say that your bravery is at best an imitation of those posturing rogues to whom I have referred.

Major, are you not convinced that everything that happens proceeds from the playfulness and daring of these people who wander in fields? Never having produced anything, neither books nor anything else useful, do they not find time enough to flood us with their babbling and baffle us with their juggling?

Canon, are you perhaps unaware of the fact that this Ernesto is descended from the great Ovid, whom you have been prodding with your forefinger?"

"Hell's teeth," replied the priest, "Do you really think, Maestro, that poetry is founded upon thievery?"

"What's all this talk about thieving?" said Antony once more. "I never noticed such things, even when they were happening right in front of me.

What I wanted to say, however, was this:

The measure of distance is the length of your walk, the measure of abundance is the extent of your hunger and foreplay precedes the event. It is also true that time in prison is measured in metre strides – Great Poet of May! It should be dactylic metre, because that's got a good rhythm for walking."

"Well, well," said the canon, wiping his forehead with a neckerchief, "I shall have to revise my opinion of you. I observe a man who stands up for the cause of poetry."

"Come off it, Canon!" came the shouted response from a shocked Antony. "Such a thought never entered my head. Canon, if I so much as hinted at such a thing, drive it right out of your mind."

CHOCKS AWAY!

Meanwhile the friends arrived at the performance area. There was already quite a gathering. Above the crowd, in a crossed swords pattern, stood two angled poles with forked tips, between which a rope had been secured. The ends of this rope were drawn down to the ground and held there by some pegs, but in a rather sloppy manner. Hugo, who'd spotted the flaw, wanted to put it right, but the canon restrained him saying:

"Pray desist, Major! A juggler's dexterity is not based on the sort of solidity you hanker after. I have a certain hidden hunch about this and my feeling is that the loose knot will redound to Ernesto's advantage."

Before the canon had finished speaking the barrel organ could be heard, a sound which through the ages has evoked the harps, drums, penny-whistles and cymbals of a choir of angels. The canon grew solemn, the major waited nonchalantly and Antony started to tap his foot.

Several women reacted impatiently, abandoning common courtesy as they elbowed their way forward. A few underage spectators escaped the crush to perch in the trees, without intending to pay any entrance fee or even bothering to keep silent.

It was approaching nine o'clock and dusk was changing to darkness. Ernesto's lamps spat a few incombustible sparks out of their sizzling interior, making them resemble the buckets into which some blacksmith had plunged red-hot bars of iron. The barrel organ was blaring, there was a rumble of anticipation in the crowd and Antony felt like breaking into song.

Meanwhile Ernesto, recognising that the numbers had stopped swelling and that it was time to get on with the performance, leapt down from the waggon and waited like a doorman for a girl, who now made her own slow descent of the steps, her face hidden by a mask.

"I have lived a life of relative tranquillity," said Antony, "and I cannot abide excitement. Isn't she pretty? Is she lacking something? God grant that she is not covering up a tumour."

"To blazes with such folly," said the canon, straining to see on the tips of his toes, "You over-zealous would-be doctor, the devil take you."

"You know what, Antony," said the major, "I see that girl has two bowls in her hands for taking the collection. When she gets to us, we'll ask her if she'll take off her mask."

"Hurrah!" said Antony, "Get a few coppers ready, Canon!"

The girl, who had no other name but Anna, passed through the lines of spectators accepting coins. They didn't fall frequently and the sound which they made revealed that they were not made of gold and that these were hard times. She ended up beneath a tree where some boys had installed themselves, and held the little bowls out to them, her limbs a straight line of pagelike poise which is the touchstone of beauty. It was evident from this action that she had perfect shoulders, a boyish chest, well-formed legs and slender hips. However, a few old women without a shred of understanding started talking as if they recognised her. "Ah, her maiden name was Shelley and her father, the one who was a terrible transgressor, knew all there was to know and composed wonderful poems."

Maintaining her charm, which seemed rather inappropriate at a moment when not even a copper was coming her way, the girl walked towards Antony, who seemed the most amiable of the three and the most likely to be generous.

"These," he declared with a bow, "are barren trees that bear no fruit. Fortunately, we are able to improve upon nature in her raw state. Gentlemen, do you have any silver at your disposal?"

The canon or the major would certainly have slipped some money to Antony, who could then have made a great show of dropping it into Anna's palm. However, the master was not a man to suffer from embarrassment. Without making any donation he tapped his finger on the metal bowl and dealt with his predicament, which clearly invited silence rather than commentary, by being all smiles.

Anna thanked all three gentlemen in a calm and courteous manner and before the major could ask her to remove her mask she did so spontaneously. She looked from one man to another, not without pleasure but without diffidence. Then she said:

"The mask is red, as you can see. It was a colour chosen quite at random, but in view of the fact that it doesn't appear to cause you displeasure, I'll stick to it."

"I was the one," answered Antony, "who registered a complaint about this manner of dressing the face. There are enough objections on grounds of health and several authors present an overwhelming number of them which is bound to persuade. However, do I have time now to list them all?"

When he had finished speaking Antony leant over and delivered a sharp and insistent whispered message into Anna's ear.

SOCIAL MISDEMEANOURS

Any book of morals worth its salt speaks out against whispering. The practice was rightly condemned in the catechisms of the church, and from that time forth people tried to avoid low tones outside a church or a public building.

When Antony committed this offence, he should have decided on a policy of silence, thus avoiding similar transgressions in the future. However, he was fated to repeat his error.

"Enough," said the major, clapping him on the shoulder. "I can see that the girl is in a hurry and cannot give us any answers."

Anna nodded in agreement. "There really isn't time and we should be getting along."

She followed these words with a sigh. And with a light touch upon Antony's elbow she and her bowls headed for a group of young men, who welcomed her into their midst just as amiably and with great courtesy.

Several old men who were standing a short distance away discussing changes in the weather left their conversation behind as they slowly and resolutely approached the performance.

As darkness was falling, circles of friends were drawing closer to the women who had arrived in short sleeves. Pleasant conversations sprang up, people marked out territory at the front and soon there was a small crowd of people, gently swaying.

Meanwhile Anna returned to the waggon and Ernesto, dressed in his fabled Flemish dancing tights, was brandishing the drumstick. So powerfully and adroitly did he make that drum roar that for forty seconds it could be heard across hill and dale. Then he flung the instrument high into the air in such a way that Anna could catch it when it fell. Scarcely had this happened before Ernesto, without any more ostentation, climbed the ladder and sat on the 'fork', where he had a pleasant perch, in order to get his breath back.

"Slow down, sir, before you overdo it," said some doubting Thomas. But he was shouted down, told to put a sock in it and reminded that the magician knew what he was doing.

At that moment the barrel organ was heard once again. With a measure of regret both canon and major became aware of Anna turning the handle. Ernesto rose to his feet and grasping the pole (which one has to hold with arm outstretched) he took an angry run along the whole length of the rope.

A TERRIBLE ART

"Such dexterity," commented Antony, "is hardly remarkable. Would you care to wager, Canon, that I could carry it off just as well without practice or preparation?"

Canon Gruntley shook his head in an expression of general lack of interest, either in the performance or the conversation. His head was thrown back and his face was radiant in contemplation of the heavenly bodies, stars and constellations, the names of which he had registered and grown familiar with.

"What you can see if you follow my finger," he pointed out, "is Sirius."

"All well and good," responded the major, "but Ernesto's going to be a falling star. See the way he has to kneel forward on the rope in order to free a calf and waggle it about. A display like this is part of a very good performance, although it's more easy to manage for those with curvature of the spine and their thigh muscles in mint condition."

Nonetheless the magician got up without so much as breaking into a sweat.

Having run up and down the rope a few times, he pulled a three-cornered hat out of a box which he'd previously prepared. Then he returned to the centre of his narrow footpath and made it vibrate unnervingly.

"Look at him," remarked the canon, turning his attention to the magician, "does he not remind you of one possessed? Does he not resemble the devil who jumps on his own tail?"

Scarcely were the words out of his lips before Ernesto, without letting up on his hip-swaying routine, began to conjure up flowers fair and fiery in flaming posies.

All these things flew out of his hat, enthralling the audience and inciting a hullabaloo of clapping and screaming and barracking, with sharp intakes of breath and gasps of fear.

"I got up very early today," commented one elderly gentleman, "but I'm not leaving until it's over because, blow me, it would be the devil's own job for this magician to avoid taking a tumble. That fellow has either got indentations in his soles and a rope plaited from a hangman's noose, or he's going to fall to earth, as they say, like a ripe tomato."

Ernesto continued at a caper, performing tricks with all his might. Despite his tiredness and drops of sweat the size of pear-shaped thumbs falling from his temple, he still had enough time to glance around and observe the major, the priest and Antony. The friends stood resting their elbows on the rim of a well, into which streams of water cascaded from the mouths of monstrous fish, sounding in the pails and marking time for the chatter of the milkmaids and the thoughts of Canon Gruntley, lost in his stargazing.

"That's them," Ernesto said to himself, and aiming at Antony's head unleashed a polyphonic burst of gunfire from his hat. Red with effort, the magician began to look almost translucent.

In short, the magician's performance was awe-inspiring and yet this was not the end of it. Quite the contrary. Exposing himself to considerable risk, he began to turn somersaults along the rope, back and forth from east to west. Only when he had made his descent and was once more back on his ladder did he stumble, almost losing his dignity as he climbed into the waggon.

IDLE SUSPICION AND AN AGREEMENT

"I am prepared to wager," said Antony, "that this fellow is deceiving us and has drawn a line somewhere, straight as an arrow, which he is using as a navigation marker. I would venture to lay odds that in this manner he made it easier to estimate the centre and that he didn't simply follow his nose in the matter, given that this particular limb is always somewhat out of kilter, be it to the left or, if not to the left, then I dare say quite conceivably to the right."

"It's clear as blazes to me," said the major, "that you're talking through your hat, Pool Captain. Did you think the somersaults weren't up to scratch?"

"If you seek perfection in somersaults," retorted Antony with a shrug of the shoulders, "then I've no means of offering you enlightenment."

At this point there was a fresh drum roll and the throng of people, rubbing the nape of their necks (because it is hard work standing with your head tilted back) began to disperse, some into blob formations and others into star shapes, the tips fashioned by the intimate weaving of strolling couples.

"The show's over. Go in peace," said the canon. And away they went.

THE MAESTRO PREPARES FOR GUARD DUTY

While at home Antony learnt that Mrs Hussey had just returned from the same performance and was intent on sleep.

"The night," he told her, staring through the window at a radiant moon, "is dark. I expect there are plenty of villains around with designs on your cushions, bath robes, towels, soap and other tools of the bathing trade. Lie down and have no fear. I will keep watch. I'll spend the night on that bed in the big bathing hut. It's hard but I don't care about that. I'll sleep lightly with one eye open."

CATHERINE AIRS HER GRIEVANCES

Once Antony had shut the door behind him, Mrs Catherine Hussey sat down on the edge of the bed, toying with her far from dainty shoe while she began to reflect:

"I can be amused by this frivolous man who's a bunch of contradictions, but when all's said and done my husband brings me grief and irritation. I am driven to unhappiness by the slightness of his brains that have shrivelled in the service of his unsavoury body. Then again there's no denying the fact that my husband snores all night and drops off without a moment's thought for the morrow. He's sleeprid-den and a tippler into the bargain."

All of a sudden several of his misdemeanours came into Mrs Hussey's mind and proved disgraceful enough to throw her into a rage. Flinging away the shoe, she began to pound the bedclothes.

"Make no bones about it," she said in the natural lan-guage of the common people, "my spirit has been wounded by his wrongs and by his woeful inadequacy. Who can hold it against me if I go hunting and foraging for one tiny expression of commitment or the merest hint of passion? Such things (and this is a constant offence) have not been provided for me by the bonds of marriage."

Then she turned to the wall with the striped bedclothes wrapped around her, a suitable emblem for a tigress, while ideas grew in her mind concerning the flawlessness of Ernesto.

She saw him smiling beneath his hat, saw him strutting along with his head hunched prettily between his shoul-ders, and lastly saw the ring flashing on his forefinger as it leant against a forehead lost in thought.

DISTURBING DREAMS

Certain vivid erotic dreams smite lovers in the depths of the night like a blow, and once they have made their appear-ance cause disturbance till break of day. This explains the fact that the sleep of lovers is intermittent and insufficient. They come round at first light, and even if they rub their eyes till tears come or count from one to a hundred and back from a thousand to fifty, they do not doze off again.

Fortunately the older schools of poetry have endowed a lover's dawn with enough beauty for those among them who appreciate the value of good literature to seek it out from time to time.

We can therefore see why Mrs Hussey lifted her shoes, slipped on a cloak and arrived at the window. It was three o'clock in the morning and the grey light of dawn had barely touched the landscape. The embankment was deserted and the Orsh dark, for night had just embedded itself in her depths.

Being in half a mind that this was a mistake and that it made no sense to be up so early, the lady opened the window onto this world.

THE HOUSE AND THE HABITS OF ANTONY

The Hussey residence formed part of a terrace of plain and hardly exceptional dwellings, and was marked out from all the others merely by a charming gutter and gates which sported a wrought-iron lock. This lock made a lot of noise when the gate was opened and closed with a key that was almost the size of an anchor. In all conscience Antony found it burdensome to carry this key around in his pocket and when he went out he used to leave the gate unlocked and his wife exposed to danger.

Mrs Hussey was well acquainted with the habits of her husband and on this occasion, when she was of a mind to go out and discovered the gate unexpectedly locked, she pounded on it with her fists and exclaimed:

"Ah the old fool, the silly ass, thinking he can lock me up and run riot without receiving his just deserts! Thinking he can shut me in and go gallivanting about all night long! Nay - even carnal knowledge is not beyond him. Because there's one thing I'm sure of, that this loathsome man has found some wanton woman and she has come to an understanding with him. Of course! No doubt about it! This is the only way his godless approach to matrimony can be explained."

THE CURSE

No sooner were the words out of her mouth than she was ready to leave. Catherine did not waste time looking for another key, because she was certain not to find it. She removed a flowerpot from the windowsill, climbed up and steeled herself to jump.

"This accursed state of matrimony," she said to herself, a fraction of her body finding space on the window sill, her legs hanging down, her dress a sad and pathetic sight as it spread itself loosely along the wall, "this accursed state has brought me nothing but injury and humiliation. Where men are concerned I could have taken my pick of the bunch, and just look at what I chose. This pileous primate, whose moustache sticks out like a weaver's yardstick caught in the mouth of a roving dog. This nincompoop, who only loves to know his dinner's waiting on a hot stove, this deflowerer foraging for foreign flora, though everything blooms for him at home!"

From thoughts such as these Catherine received the impulse to action. She leapt down and despite the fact that the wall beneath was far from high, she landed on her hands. However the minor grazing which she received and instantly considered a calamity drove her to new heights of fury.

THOSE MAGNIFICENT YEARS, THE NINETIES

It was the year 1891 and in a community near to the eastern border of Bohemia the harvest was bountiful where the spud is concerned. There were so many of them that no end of waggons were juddering under their weight and not even two pairs of bullocks, cows and other beasts of burden could transport them all.

"Alas!" came the word from the farmers, each one with a sharp nose rearing up from beneath a peaked cap, "Alas!

Alack! We have been struck by times of plenty! The devil take them! Winter's waiting in the wings, isn't it! It'll freeze on the spot, the lot of it! We'll all go to rack and ruin!"

"Oh, oh, woe! Who will come to our aid? Who will take care of us? Who will restore our fortunes?"

"What's all this?" answered a good-natured old Jew, a trader in the fruits of the fields, "what have you made such a mess of now, my dears?"

Nevertheless, when the countrymen bravely held out for what was due to them, he rendered it in gold coins.

No sooner had this happened and the farmers had their hands on money, than they began to hanker after pleasant diversions, such as befitted and were appropriate to their property and their new standing in society.

They would doubtless have been tracked down with their heads in refined works of literature or in glasses around the pubs, had it not been for a farmer by the name of Benedict Gherkin, who set a bad example to them all. He took a fancy to a widow, showered her with favours and money, and allocated her a monthly pension of twenty pieces of gold.

Then Mrs Gherkin, never to be forgotten and an object lesson for all husbands errant, courageously threw on her glad rags and approached the governor of their community, who had not planted enough potatoes, and persuaded him to summon both miscreants to a hearing. The widow wayward and the husband errant.

When they arrived the wife flew into a rage and began to shout in a voice clear and sonorous: "See the shameless wench! Look at him, the profligate!"

She wrung her hands and pierced the mayoral soul with her weeping. Many kind words were needed from the governor in order to calm her down. However, no sooner were they out of his mouth and no sooner had she mastered her grief (her eyes still glistening from the recent tide of tears) than she started to slap the wily widow about the cheeks, both facial and fundamental, and on the fetching dimple displayed on her chin. She treated her husband's jaw to a heavy stroke with an ancient carving confirming the rights of mayoralty, which she managed to tear from its position hanging on the wall, and proceeded to whack, pound and pummel, lashing out wildly and knocking the living daylights out of them.

"Enough!" interceded the mayor, noting that a full half hour had passed by, "we are not young any more, let us forgive one another. What do you say to the idea that we kiss and make up."

With these words he proceeded to kiss the widow.

When Farmer Gherkin arrived home, he lay down without demanding anything to eat or drink, notwithstanding the fact that it was close to noon. However, his wife, ever mindful of how she had been betrayed and damaged, once her tears had dried out in her wrinkles and in the small folds of her tidy double chin, clung to him and pressured him unceasingly, until he apologised and promised her that he would mend his ways.

This incident is common knowledge, although the quick-tempered Mrs Hussey did not allow herself the patience to draw the kernel of wisdom from the nut of ancient folklore.

So the kernel stayed in the nut and the marrow remained wedged inside the bone.

Walking by the willows, Catherine overheard sighs which evidently hadn't come from the throat of Antony. She quickened her step.

Luna, Star of Lovers, radiated moonbeams onto the scene, birds cheeped in the undergrowth and all the auguries were for a beautiful day in the making.

But Mrs Hussey was beyond noticing. Short and furious steps marked her journey to the bridge, which she crossed with unsteady legs, before reaching the door of the large cabin in which Antony's bed was to be found.

Many a maxim is devoted to ways of soothing someone's anger and controlling violent fits of temper, but the wife of the bathing superintendent failed to bring any to mind, just as she omitted to take into account the story of the spuds.

Two voices could be heard on the other side of the door, and seeing that only one of the two could belong to Antony, Mrs Hussey pounded on the door shouting at the top of her voice:

"Open up! Open, you depraved and shameless philanderer! Open, libertine, or I will break the door down!"

With these words she really began to search for a pick-axe, a crowbar or a hatchet.

THE ETERNAL MOMENT

Silence fell upon the inside of the cabin. A blood-curdling moment went by during which Catherine's heart managed ninety beats.

All of a sudden there was the sound of something falling and an unmistakable tinkling of glass.
"Heavens above!" the woman exclaimed, "You've been at the bottle! Gentlemen! Is that you? Major, is that you, sir? Canon, is that you in there, reverend sir?"

From time immemorial an old chair had been standing beside the entrance to the pool area. As she was in a flurry of movement she was too late in noticing it and caught her knee joint on the chair edge. Not a single oath passed her lips as she gathered this item of furniture into her arms and carried it to the cabin door. No sooner had she put the chair in position than she was already climbing onto it, securing her footing by clasping the upper boards of the cabin, and eagerly raising her splendiferous body to a height which would enable her to peep through the opening above the door into the interior of the cabin.

THERE YOU ARE!

This was the cue for Antony to open the door.

"Quick! No time to lose!" he insisted, keeping a straight face despite the fact that water was streaming from his trousers, "what are you waiting for, why are you still hanging around here? Run! Get moving! Bring this poor girl a smidgen of warm milk and some dry undergarments. I'm afraid that she's been under too long."

"What are you on about," rejoindered the pool manager's wife as she approached Antony's bed, on which Anna was resting with eyes rolled upwards and shirt glued to her pink body.

"Lord love a duck, she's had a soaking," she added, after a moment of silence in which she ran her eyes in an unceremonious manner over the girl, Anna's loveliness now transparent.

WISE UP!

The following day the canon and the major descended on the Isle of Hussey, making inquiries of Antony concerning the night's drownings and rescues.

"Well now," said the impresario, in between snatches of song, (seeing that Catherine had gone off to do the shopping), "I pulled a poor little scrap out of the Orsh, a slip of a girl who hadn't seen 21.

Gentlemen, she would have been a drowned rat."

"Some chatter came to my ears at breakfast today," put in the canon. "It informed me, Antony, that this little scrap was Anna, the girl from the magician's waggon, and that you dragged her here through the willows. This unfortunate young lady, Major, was apparently forced to cast herself into the depths in order to escape the attentions of a reprobate. You are silent, Antony. Does this mean that you consent to being publicly proclaimed a seducer and branded a scoundrel?"

"Spot on," retorted the major, "Nothing wrong with a pretty girlfriend, I should know it. Rosy little mouth and ears."

Touched with emotion, the major followed his speech with a moment of silence. Then he continued: "I say I should know it, but time never stops and we forget things."

"As for you, Antony," he went on, turning to the master of the lido, "your behaviour is worse than a mercenary pillaging a conquered town. The padre has every right to call you a scoundrel."

"There was no unpleasantness hidden in my escapade," explained Antony. "Anna is still with us. She breathes, she moves. I promised her some fish. As for you, Major, you should give me a helping hand because, as I noticed when I stole a glance at her, she really is an attractive girl."

ENOUGH

Hearing these words the canon extracted Ovid's Ars Amandi from his pocket and flung the book onto the ground, where it stirred up a cloud of dust.

Then the priest launched into a diatribe and spoke scathingly of literature and books. He claimed that poets were timid creatures whose craft was not held in high esteem. Women treat them like foot-rags.

When his sermonette was over he retrieved his book and continued:

"If I have been remonstrating against the beauties of literature, I do not say that my remarks admit of no qualification or are generally applicable. However, it is irrefutably the case that women are feeble-minded. They have never to any degree taken part in great things or tasted spiritual pleasures."

"Just what I say," remarked the major while he lit a cigar. "They know nothing of military service. However much they go for the tight trousers and colourful coats, they don't have a clue about soldiering. You know what, Padre, I have yet to meet a woman who knew the first thing about ballistics or tactics, or who could even offer an opinion about these things.

With the utmost ease," he added, throwing in a 'humph', "they manage to bring ruin to ancient family lines. It's their cross-breeding with the offspring of aristocracy. The end product is a world hooked on penny dreadfuls."

HELL HATH NO FURY...

Meanwhile Mrs Hussey sorted out the larder and made her way back to the Orsh. Antony spotted her coming and at once launched himself into a flurry of tidying up. He seized hold of a pail, scooped up some water and spread it around on the pool platform. Then he grabbed a twist of rope and began mopping up the puddles he'd created, devoting all his strength to the task.

"That man," complained Mrs Hussey, "is my husband, a man who betrays his wife! This very night I caught him in bed with a girl."

"Was the girl not wet?" came the defence from Antony.

"Wet she was," Mrs Hussey repeated, "but listen to me while I explain what happened.

In the master cabin there is a basin full of water. And in this very basin, Major, or we could call it a tub if you prefer, Canon, we keep the bottles which we have for sale, preserving them at the right temperature and ensuring that the contents are fresh."

While Mrs Hussey was offering this detailed description of the means of storage and trading practices essential to the art of victualling, she was once again at the door which she had approached that morning, and in a re-run of her earlier activities she subjected it to a fresh pounding.

"I heard a crash, a sound of glass breaking and of trickling water, I heard that too. Now I have the terrible truth before my very eyes. Now it is unfortunately all too clear that this water came from Antony's trousers and that the adulterer sat in the basin only in order to pull the wool over my eyes and deceive me. The shamelessness of it! They soaked their shirts and underclothes to serve their treachery."

WHO COULD IT HAVE BEEN?

"That would be a wicked and unforgivable act of betrayal," vouchsafed the canon. "I ask you, however, to take a look at Antony. Do you really think it's likely that this numskull could find favour with such an enchanting girl? Are you quite sure that you're not mistaken? Are you certain it was the magician Anna you laid eyes upon?"

"Canon Gruntley's quite right," put in the major. "Perhaps it was some grimalkin back from a spot of mushrooming or wood-gathering. You know what, madam, it could be that Antony really did haul her out of the Orsh. After all, how can you be certain that things happened the way you say they did and that Antony really made hay with this girl? Your husband used to be a reprobate, but time's caught up with him since then."

"No one knows better than I do how old he is," the maestro's wife replied. "I know perfectly well that this drab did not come from mushrooming or from wood-gathering. She came from the waggon. You hit the nail right on the head. Anna it was."

"I say!" exclaimed the major. "See how Mrs Hussey leads the charge from the lido. That virago of yours will tan the girl's hide. Look at the speed of the woman. Can you see the fumes?"

"My wife," put in Antony, "is unhinged and a vicious harridan. There's nothing for it but to take my cap and stick and go after her. I fear there's nothing else to be done. I shall be compelled to hammer the sense back into her."

GAME WITH GROATS

The centrepiece of Little Karlsbad is a solid main square, lined with substantial houses. Here you will find an abundance of lawns, several trees and a fountain. Two pleasant pathways flanking a large brewery connect the square to a park, which they run through before ascending a delightful hillock, perched on which you'll find the church dedicated to St. Lawrence. It is said that in times gone by there was a monastery here and that the monks were more than fond of a tipple. From the time when the monastery was founded, a hawthorn hedge has bordered the paths leading to the basilica. Here and there along the route you will find benches which receive a fresh coat of paint every spring.

Having come to this spot Antony sat down on one of the benches, so that he could not be observed from Ernesto's waggon, but at the same time had a reasonably good view of what was going on there. The magician's abode was located at a fork in the main road, where waggon, rope, trapeze and carpet were all to be found.

Antony listened out, but all around reigned silence, ease and tranquillity.

"Evidently," he said, "my wife changed her mind and is going to leave Anna alone. The passing of two hours must have taken the sting out of her rage or at least have blunted its edges."

Having voiced this opinion he began to eye up the waggon in a different and more daring manner. However, the door remained shut and Anna was nowhere to be seen. A few tales of yesteryear floated through the maestro's mind while, on the verge of nodding off, he fiddled with a few groats which he'd come across in his pocket.

THE GREEN WAGGON

"Time to take a walk," he told himself, driving an unwelcome drowsiness out of his mind. With these words he got up and headed towards the travelling home.

He walked around the waggon, unable to detect any signs of life. He lifted up the magician's drumstick, suspended himself from the trapeze, ran his hand along the pole and stroked the dog, noticing the hunger in it and the fact that it had a limp. When he had finished working on the environs, he began to examine the things that were hanging on the outside of the waggon: a yoke, a pan of some sort and, to round things off, a couple of hens. The birds were tied together at the leg and attached to a peg. Three colours were on display in the wings hanging at their sides.

"My God!" exclaimed Mr Hussey as he inspected the fowls carefully from close up, "These are very similar to the ones which go bustling about in our courtyard. I'd be very interested to know whether the hen has had her wings clipped and whether the little cock has a copper ring on its right leg.

Ah ha!" he cried out on coming across two very revealing signs, namely a cross engraved on the copper and the uneven character of the wing-clipping.

He proceeded to pick up a stick and after subjecting the thick window to a tapping went off giving full vent to loud guffaws. It seemed to him that the last shred of circumspection had abandoned Mrs Catherine Hussey, a woman so well cushioned about the middle, one who glowed with perspiration and always quarrelled so violently. "These are the great and grievous muddlings that come with advancing age," he pronounced. "This is love coming on the cusp of two seasons in one's life. I can just see my corpulent but respectable wife pursuing chickens around the courtyard, can see the look of reluctance as she cuts their throats, can see her placing them head down on the roof of the chicken coop, can see her flush as she bears them under her apron to lay them at Ernesto's feet. I forgive her everything, I wouldn't bat an eyelid about any of it, but I would like to be assured that her affections for him are strong and constant.

Be off with you, lovebirds," he added, "fly off arm in arm, take to your heels, spread your wings and for God's sake never come back!"

BEWARE OF THE GUARDS!

At dinnertime the next day the town constable cut himself a slice of bread, ate the cheese in his customary manner and took a drink. Then he rose to his feet, seized hold of the sharp weapon at his side and ventured out onto the street.

"Just you remember," he said to the children playing on the edge of the pavement, "that we should always keep to the right hand side. Just remember that, you young hooligans, or I'll give you what for till you won't know what's happened to you."

The reprimand being over, and having remembered his own childhood years, he waved his arm and duly turned his mind towards attending the magician's performance. And this was the moment when the major arrived with the priest and Antony, and proceeded to grab hold of him by a strap.

"Sir," he began brusquely, without paying him more courtesies than were due to his position, "Sir, while you have been quaffing in The Green Maiden, while you have been neglecting your official duties, the property of a citizen has been pillaged. To calculate the theft precisely, there are two chickens missing in this town."

"There you are," the constable came back, "there you are, then. Does your chicken coop have a lock or is it without one? Was it left open or shut?"

"It was open," explained Antony, "because this was a case of daylight robbery."

A CASE OF SINGING

"So much the worse," came the follow-up from the constable, "whoever steals during daylight hours is a scoundrel twice over. In any case, you know what, Gentlemen? I knew one degenerate whose behaviour in these matters was even worse. He ventured out for his acts of plunder at noon with a cheerful song on his lips. Of course a person like that could never mend his ways."

"Perverse and reprehensible as such behaviour is," the man of God intervened, "do you not realise that there is always time for a soul to repent and that whosoever brings a contrite heart to the remembrance of his offences, whosoever regrets his misdeeds and unburdens himself of them in the confessional, shall receive forgiveness? I have an enduring hope in regard to your yokel that he will not be a lost soul, of course on the understanding that there was nothing immoral in what he was singing and that he turns over a new leaf."

"I don't know the words of the song," said the constable, "because he was a crafty devil and we never managed to lay hands on him."

"You haven't got a hard case like that here," intervened the major, "the master's hens went off without any singing."

"So it's you," declared the constable, turning to face Antony, "you're the one implicated in this theft!"

After which he went off, nodding his head.

THE SKIES ARE CLEAR

From all corners of the town the inhabitants came hurrying to the performance, and by the time the three friends had arrived in the square it was packed. The drum and whistling sounded more melodious than they had the day before because of the clear conditions, and the stars twinkled in the heavens above.

"The nights," opined Antony, "are markedly fine, but it all comes to nothing during the day. Why do you think that is, Canon?"

"My view," replied the priest, "is that you are a great sinner and this inclemency during daylight hours is a punishment from on High."

"Balderdash," retorted Antony, "there were times when we spent every minute God gave sinning and it never stopped the sun shining. Our sins are not the issue."

GOOD MANNERS

Some adolescent boys were engaged in every kind of teasing dalliance with the girls. Wild ideas fermented in their heads and they couldn't get their eyes off the opposite sex. Antony counted about ten of them. The damsels kept looking back at them through the narrowed eyes of prey swooning with pleasure. Spine-tingling tremors ran down their backs, and whenever they replied to their friends they clapped their palms over their mouths. Antony, the canon and the major, perched once more on the edge of the fountain some distance off the ground, enjoyed an unobstructed view of these capers, because everything was out in the open and plain to see.

"Affection between the two sexes," pronounced Antony, "goes back further than the rocks and the seven seas and yet, Canon, this does not mean the coming of the deluge, oh no. Behold these friendships old and newly minted," he continued, pointing with the major's stick from one pair to another, "do you not consider them desirable and pleasing to God? Do you not feel an urge to become part of it all, to have contact and make connection with this creative force, even if that would place you on a collision course with the Contemplative Order of Carthusians?"

The canon's head began to move and appeared to register a nod of agreement.

GIRL WITH A TIN PLATE

Meanwhile it was high time for Anna, the magician's girl, to pay attention to her bowls. All manner of charm went into her descent from the waggon, after which she started to tap on a tin plate with a rosy finger, as Antony Hussey had done the day before, and jingled the coins as she went from man to man and from girl to woman, not forgetting the nippers and dodderers.

"Antony, dear sir," was her address to Mr Hussey in front of the fountain, "Dear sir, I am so very much obliged to you and thank you for the assistance you gave me."

"Well, well," came the reply, "You seem to be of a very delicate nature. Has nothing happened to render you indisposed? You haven't caught a cold?"

"Oh," she responded, "I took a cupful of tea and your dear wife, Mrs Hussey, dealt with me for hours."

"My wife is given to futile and angry tirades," answered Antony, putting his arm around the girl's waist.

"Let her remain in Ernesto's little ark," he added, "but you should not be going back there."

"Oh," replied Anna, "Ernesto may be a magician of the middle rank only, but his skills as a foster father leave nothing to be desired."

A moment later, having accepted money from no one but the major, she was lost in the crowd.

MYSTERIOUS MUSIC

"Mark their tricks of magic well," said Antony, holding up three fingers. "Ernesto is standing in front of his shack, Anna is going round collecting money and yet our ears can testify to the fact that the barrel organ keeps on playing. I'm afraid the devil must be in the service of that magician."

"I've often supposed that you lacked horse sense, and I see that my fears were not groundless. How can you joke about your wife deserting you?" observed Hugo.

A SECOND PERFORMANCE

No sooner was this discussion over than Ernesto, accompanied by a roll on the drums, began to cry out that the performance was about to begin. Then he climbed carefully onto the tightrope and performed a few strange and incredible turns. Gradually he changed into a devil, a matchstick, a clown, a monkey, the thief of Baghdad, a small apple, a hobnail, a university beadle, a drunkard, a lunatic and his final metamorphosis, standing right on the very edge, was into the form of a preacher vociferating that there were people at the back with eyes coming out of their sockets who had failed to pay.

Having taken a breather he perched himself prettily on the tips of his forefingers and then, with these fingers bearing the whole of his bodily weight, he crossed the rope to loud applause and cheering.

"A live wire, that 'un." "Works till 'e drops." "'E's one as knows the ropes." So said several newcomers from the surrounding villages, who in their enthusiasm used the forms of speech, turns of phrase and images of common parlance.

MONSOON IN A GLASS

At the approach of ten o'clock Ernesto fetched a small table, lit four lamps and prepared a few tricks and examples of the magician's art. The table was bare, the hands of the magician were empty and yet at the click of his fingers a magnificent example of uncut glass full of water appeared in the middle of the table. No sooner had Ernesto clapped his hands, puffed out his cheeks and blown than the water in the glass began to swirl and spill itself onto the ground in a powerful and protracted flow.

If these antics had continued any longer, the whole town could have been under water, because this uncut wellhead, otherwise known as a monsoon in a glass, had a yield of 129 hectolitres per hour. This figure corresponds exactly to what is borne by the pipes delivering the town's current water supply.

"All well and good," the audience came back at him, "turn off the tap and don't bother us with things like this. We are not short of rainfall here, thank God. Haven't we been soaked to the skin all day, not to mention all day yesterday?"

ENTERTAINMENT COMES IN MANY GUISES

When the production was over, Ernesto bowed prettily and disappeared into the waggon. The audience dispersed homewards. A few of them stopped off in the pubs where some drank a glass of stout or three, while others opted for the ales from Budweis. Another contingent headed for the orchard and a further group to the meadows, though here the dampness was inhibiting.

Antony yawned and explained to the major that he was tired and off for some sleep.

"Time we were going," agreed Hugo, "Eleven o'clock waiting to strike."

"Oh indeed," added the canon, "I shall stay in the square for a little while. I would like to see how Ernesto makes his bed and how he lies down in it. I would so like to know what arrangement will be made concerning those two females, because the vehicle is small and it is my opinion that it does not sport three bedrooms."

"Do you know how to whistle through your fingers?" inquired Antony, "Well then, if something unsavoury happens to you, whistle with all your strength."

CONVERSATION AT NIGHT

The canon paced up and down the pavements and was just at the point where he was making one of his repeated approaches to the waggon, when he observed its little door opening and two people stepping down from it. One of them was slight and the other, judging from volume, strongly reminiscent of Mrs Hussey.

"I can see and recognise," said canon Gruntley to himself, "the thin calves and the crooked thighs of the magician. I can see that good lady is going to fall into sin." Then he extracted a book from his pocket and taking it in his hand he approached Ernesto's abode. The window shone with a reddish glow.

"This very day," he said, when the little window had opened slightly, "time and tide have already failed to wait. I should have been more careful and I should have given you this book at the very beginning, seeing that it contains beautiful narratives and several modest love stories which would be suitable for your hearing."

"If you will allow me a moment," replied Anna, "I have some fish in the frying-pan and I'm afraid that I might burn the dinner."

"It is quite pointless to fuss about such things," insisted the canon, "The fish are not fresh and it is not a day for fasting."

"In that case," replied Anna, "I will open up for you and you can be the one to turn the pan nicely over the fire."

AT THE GREEN MAIDEN

Inside the hostelry which enjoyed this charming appellation, a few hardened drinkers had gone one over the eight. Being of an argumentative and quarrelsome disposition, they started yelling at the pubkeeper that his beer was the piss of the gnat and his food spiced to hide a similar provenance.

"Wait a moment, waddler, are you trying to annoy us? What is this metal dish for? Will you make us pay for cards too? You tosspot, you tradesman odious and malodorous!"

When all this had been spoken and their submissions had finally drawn to a close, they put down their cards and off they went into the square. Here they walked to and fro until their wanderings finally delivered them to the magician's waggon, at which point they started to move it, propelling it this way and that, kicking away the linchpin, treating the dog's haunches to a slapping, the window to a pounding, the sides to a drumming, Ernesto to a cry of 'you old ape' and Anna to repeated offers of marriage.

THE BATTLE OF THE GREEN WAGGON

One of these people, by the name of Peterson, climbed up the ladder to the window and opened it, poking his head inside. However, before he could take a look around he received such a sharp blow to the ear that his eyes were forced shut. This was followed up with a fist to the depresor, a third blow to the levator and a fourth to the buccinator. After this he gave a howl and fell under the waggon.

When the others saw their companion suffer such humiliation, they flew into a rage. They broke down the door and forced their way into the waggon, smashed dishes and threw a tantrum of thumping, ranting and raving. The commotion was enough to waken the town constable in The Fourteen Helpers. Scarcely had this old soldier managed to put his belt on before he was hurrying towards the scene of the disturbance, a pipe burning between his teeth and the seven of hearts in his cupped hand.

Meanwhile the canon escaped the mêlée and on hearing that the constable was being summoned he broke the nearest streetlight. This enabled him to submerge himself in darkness. He waited for an opportune moment and then made his escape along a wall, before scurrying across the square and turning into Lord Mayor's Street, from which he skedaddled home.

EPISCOPAL CIRCUMSPECTION

People whose minds are feeble or muddied by their own folly are never in a state of contentment, but wisdom brings assurance. The wise strut about with their hands behind their backs and taking into account the things eternal they are not to be hurried in assessing a misadventure.

Some bishop of Bognor Regis was an irrepressible enthusiast for the hunting of hare, in the pursuit of which he displayed a great talent. Deep inside shady groves, out in the sun, over fields of potatoes or stubble, he'd go hunting through them all. On a meticulously apparelled steed he assumed a comely posture of uprightness and rode along the drainage channel between fields, meditating on the thrill of the chase with his huntsman, who followed about a horse's length behind him.

"Festina lente," he used to say, "haste not speed, huntsman! The hare is a small and nimble creature. We on the other hand are grown men given to prudence. Only the foolish go bearing down on the skitterer, turning red, turning purple, struggling to catch their breath, while one who has thought the matter over proceeds slowly. Let this lagomorph make his escape, I wager that any minute now another will spring forth and whether you believe me or not, whether they all start running or all the game has gone to ground in holes, we will still be dining on hare tonight."

LESSONS LEARNED FROM BOOKS AND THOSE WHICH COME FROM CONVERSATIONS

Antony, master of the bathing arena, could be distinguished from his wife by the fact that she was a blatherskite, whereas he had the ability, at the appropriate time, to make mental use of the experiences of other people. Thinking of the bishop he remarked to the major:

"It's plain to me that my wife will accompany Ernesto to the ends of the earth. It is clear that last night the canon climbed into Anna's waggon where he fawned upon her and made full use of his facility of expression (whose boundlessness we are well aware of) in the cause of bewitching her; but there are many fish in the sea!

Wisdom walks hand in hand with age. Mrs Hussey has clocked up forty-five years in respectable company and has improved her mind listening to your speeches; I am quite sure that she knows what she's doing, that she weighed all the pros and cons before deciding to go and that she realised what little she has in the way of virtue. This canon, on the other hand, has sunk to the depths of debauchery."

"I was with him this very morning," said the major, "he has some laceration about the ear and a swollen face. Reading two books and keeping his pecker up."

"Well, well, keeping his pecker up!" repeated Antony. "Perhaps he broke out in song? He surely cannot but be aware – indeed you, Major, cannot but be aware – that the whole town is up and about and that the only thing on any Tom, Dick or Harry's lips is the reverend's night raising Cain. I think that a mark of contrition is called for, such as might be inflicted by the flagellant's whip, as in all the best monasteries. Is he not a professional of the cloisters?"

"He is not," replied Hugo, "and it ill becomes a man like you to offer advice on such unsavoury things. He's already paid the price for his misdemeanour. He's got an earlobe hanging on to the rest of his face by a sliver of skin and if you ask me it needs a stitch or two to persuade it to stay. Knuckle down to it with your needle."

"Certainly," said Antony, "I'd be only too happy to help out, but that doesn't mean I approve of his sinful behaviour."

With these words the bathing superintendent began to look for the right material for sewing up wounds, and having rummaged through several cupboards he finally found it. There was a fine-looking needle with a good shine on it that had once been a fish hook, and some silk thread which is good for fishing when attached to a lead weight. Antony twisted the silk thread around his finger, took the needle in the tips of his fingers and without bothering himself over the state of the swimming pool went out behind the major, who was pressed for time.

THE FIELD SURGEON INTERVENES

The canon's residence stood in the midst of a shady garden, access to which was procured by means of a small gate. The friends passed through it. As they headed along the footpath towards the house, a couple of small, bandy-legged pooches hightailed by. Master Hussey pointed at them and said that the canon must take pleasure in freaks of nature. Conversing loudly they made their way up the steps.

"The doctor," commented the major, when they had exchanged greetings with the canon, "would spread tittle tattle about you in pubs. When visit-ing patients he'd speak at great length about what was wrong with you. It's a habit of people in the medical profession to make a great song and dance about things, Gruntley, but let's face it, it's not as if you lost your ear upholding the truth of the gospel, besides which it's better to keep mum about this. So Mr Hussey will take charge of your treatment.

You don't need me to speak highly of him. You know yourself that he has a deft and careful hand when it comes to needles and pricks."

"Antony Hussey," came the response from the priest, "is a gifted person. Will you take some wine, Gentlemen?"

"I will indeed need some," responded the master life-guard, "some alcohol or a saucepan of boiling water in order to remove the grime, which seems to me to be of a certain age, from my equipment. Bring it here, Canon."

When the implements had been sterilised, Antony rolled up his sleeves and having carefully scrubbed his hands nine times in water he began to encourage a spirit of forbearance on the part of the canon by shouting:

"Just be of good cheer, reverend sir, be of good cheer! Don't be so threatening! Hold out the ear with heroic resolution and for God's sake don't come out with any profanities or you'll confuse me."

Four stitches were necessary. The master cleaned the wound and then made the stitches, piercing four times with a skilful swish through both edges of the wound, leading the thread through them and tying a knot. Then he dressed the wound in a charming lace handkerchief and secured it with a clerical collar.

A PECULIAR VIEW CONCERNING SCRAPS

"This little adventure of yours," said the major sitting himself down, "seems to have turned unexpectedly into a scrap. I'd never have thought it. You've been in the wars, Padre, but just how did it come about?"

"Oh," replied the priest, "you know that I retreat from any fray and you should realise that if I have a torn ear it is not because I would ever change my approach."

THE PERCH

"I stopped in the square and meeting no objections I began to strike up a conversation with Anna, who was preparing a dinner of fried fish."

"Did you join her in eating this meal?" inquired Antony, his face a picture of gloom.

"I sampled some perch," replied the canon, "and it was the very fish that you had pulled out of the Orsh yesterday at midday."

"That's enough," came the further retort from Antony, who proceeded to fly into a rage (because he couldn't bear the idea that the canon had dined on his own fish with Anna), "Enough, keep your shameful little saga to yourself. It is not a subject fit for my ears. I know it already.

O the ways of the poet-roué! O the ways of literature!"

OF ACCURSED LITERATURE

"When will a tale of respectable mental anguish come to my ears again? When will I read about deep inner strivings? When will fiction emerge from the brothel? When will it cease to sing about plain and humdrum topics? When will it turn its attention to the nobility of civic virtue?

When will I find in your books at least a single page about buying and selling, a page which treats of the ill effects of bankruptcy, a page about love of one's country, the sale of cattle and drainage projects? When will they publish the new Georgics? When will they bring out a book of poems about physical strength and the nuts and bolts of campaigning for one's class in the true sense of that term? When will it happen and how remote is that time from us now?

I have heard you spouting verses with no didactic value, verses foaming at the metre with blood and the inhumanity of a professional who imposes a new and incomprehensible beauty upon the world at the cost of hunger and forgetting the past. All the major and I have to say about it is that it is pointless and profane.

Night after night you have been looking for a way of referring to what doesn't exist and searching out an expression which is all too common on the lips of yokels. You, huntsman for words, have used the resources of the whole world in order to produce one short, broken sentence, oblivious to the real stories which your neighbours have to tell.

You used language neither familiar nor famous, and in all this your morals have sunk low enough to get you into scraps."

THE CANON MAKES A CONFESSION

"Yes," came the response from the man of God, "I received a wound and you stitched me up. It is also true that I used to have books with me on my walks beside the Orsh and that I used to take them with me to the lido. Shakespeare, Rabelais and Cervantes, they were all my companions; I would be willing to put my head on the block for them, just as I put my ear on the block for Anna."

"Well now," commented the major, "the only fair and noble death is the one that comes on the battlefield, but poets tend to be poor soldiers. The pool captain is quite right."

INSIDE THE WAGGON

At around five on the same day a roll of thunder could be heard over the heights defining the Northern boundary of the Little Karlsbad valley basin. It seemed that a storm was about to strike.

"Take note," said the citizens, "there is no surer law of nature than the law of St. Swithin's Day. Indeed a drop of rain that falls that day, for forty days won't go away. That's the truth. It's been fine weather so far today, but the louring clouds mean rain at any moment. That Ernesto's in for a drenching."

WOMEN ARE ALWAYS THE SAME

The magician was sitting on a bench, watching through the window and pondering the likely eventuality of rain with displeasure.

"My dear lady," he remarked to Catherine while she carefully applied a needle to a hole in his jacket, "I ran into a snow storm once, wintering in the Tyrol. Conditions hyperborean, waggon frozen through, little chimney not unlike this one unable to draw air. A great mountain range pervades the Tyrolean landscape, with snow recumbent on the peaks and a whistling North wind."

DISCOMFORT

"Oh dear me," came the reply from Mrs Hussey, interrupting her needlework, "you've been to the very ends of the earth and you've lived through enough and to spare of bad weather. Praise be to God that on a day like this, rain though it may, it does not freeze and this stove works well enough."

"Goes without saying," Ernesto pursued the point, "but at that time there was a snowstorm and all the passes were blocked."

"I would like to ask you," returned the lady, interrupting his narration, "whether you could keep a clean waggon in such circumstances, because a tidy home is a happy one and makes a long stay inside endurable and pleasant. When I've repaired this coat and patched up your underclothes, I have it in mind to produce some rugs and cushions. Items like these, Ernesto, provide the icing on the cake in any dwelling."

"That would be swell," responded the magician, "but don't forget the carpet which we use during our performance. Anna burnt right through it with a cigarette and now it has a hole bigger than the palm of your hand."

"Only yesterday I reprimanded her. That girl is a wilful wrecker of our things. She'd better not play with fire! She'd better not provoke me, or I'll send her packing and she won't even get the term of notice maids are entitled to," replied Mrs Hussey.

Meanwhile the rain began to fall. Huge drops cascaded off the windows and buffeted the roof of the waggon. Already oblivious to what Catherine was saying, the magician's eyes were fixed on the thickening gloom of twilight outside. The shadows of approaching night interposed themselves between Ernesto and this conscientious woman. The magician was listening to the howling wind and the pitter-patter of rain. This was the moment when it seemed to him that somewhere inside his body, in some entrail none could fathom, the mysterious voice of regret was suddenly sounding its call.

ANTONY'S CONVERSION

"Sir," began the major as he approached Antony, "Weather this evening's nothing to write home about."

"You're right there," Antony agreed, "I can't see Ernesto even crawling out of his waggon in conditions like this. Your trip to the performance will be all for nothing."

"So," the major came back again, "I can see what sort of a stay-at-home you are, Antony. A man who's lost his temper and dug his heels in. Has a girl never before given you the heave-ho? Haven't a few walked out on you? Stop being bitter and smoke a peace pipe with the canon, who is no more than the handmaid of Providence.

Have you forgotten how we used to go along the Orsh rootling around in the earth below bushes of box thorn, beneath dog rose and blackthorn and under brambles where the earthworms lurked, those lovers of moisture in the soil?

All those congenial talks which made the hours fly by! Evenings spent over a fishing line, when keeping a weather eye on the float. At that time you were all ears for those pretty and polished canonical speeches! Those verbal spats, so charming and captivating, which always came to a fine conclusion!

We can have all this again! Get your coat, Antony, and let's go."

"It pleases me," the master responded with a smile, "to have the benefit of your words of wisdom and to be able to discern the truth of them. Upon my soul, sir, it was a poor show that I became so hot under the collar simply because the canon has a liking for attractive girls. For he always was a lady-killer, just like you, the man preparing to supplant him in the saddle.

But let us not dwell on anything unpleasant. Of course the canon didn't have to polish off the perch, but let's forgive him for doing so."

Having delivered himself of these words Antony rose from his seat and treated the major to a hug followed by a pat on the back.

Chatting together in the manner of times past, they made their way to the square, arriving at the very moment when the rain was easing off.

Quite a few people had congregated in the passageways and beside the houses on the North side of the square. The plane-trees dripped incessantly and dusk billowed out in the square like a banner of mourning. The magician didn't seem too keen on performing and lethargy stalked his female assistant.

"I have said it before," master Hussey began, "and I will say it again a thousand times. Anna is not suited to a place like this. Look at the awkward way in which she conducts herself. Look at the way she scours those bowls for money that isn't there."

"I think that you should marry her, Major, because the likelihood is that she has received nothing but torment from Mrs Hussey."

"Miss," he went on to say, as Anna came towards him, "tie your things up in a bundle and leave the waggon to fend for itself. Come and join us! Take over my spa facilities and the books of the canon."

"But what will we do with the major?" asked the girl.

"I will dispatch the magician and go to prison," offered Hugo.

At this moment, just in the nick of time, Ernesto seized hold of the bugle and blew with all his might. Nevertheless the sound was more like groats falling out of a sack.

WINE AND BALDERDASH - THE RECIPE

After you've enjoyed a glass of wine after work, it may occur to you sometimes that you could lift up a paving stone or two and hurl them one after another at the street lamps.

Sometimes there is time to spare for balderdash. From time to time it does happen that some august prince of the Church splits his sides laughing, while he repeats over and over again a joke or ditty gleaned from the suburbs.

All to the good. A person loses no respect by laughing (unless he should laugh too long). But woe betide those laborious jesters who strain and sweat for three days preparing their tricks, just so that they can then hold out a hat, a sheet of music or a saucer.

Heaven help Ernesto, who lingered too long in Little Karlsbad.

A POOR LEVEL OF ATTENDANCE

The square was almost deserted, but the wretched magician kept traversing the high wire turning somersaults, pushing a wheelbarrow, lifting and bending his legs.

"Well", said Antony, "No applause, no whoops of delight. I'm afraid that nothing would put life into this lot. Not even a monsoon in a glass. Not even gunfire, or better still the sound of a fart from Ernesto's hat."

THE THIRD PERFORMANCE

Meanwhile the magician was balancing on the big toe of his right foot and whirling around on the vertical axis of his spinning body. And it was right at this moment, when all the ardour of the performer was being invested in his act, that a grandpa full of Dutch courage, stick in hand and head nodding, emerged from The Green Maiden and proceeded to stand under the magician's tightrope,
where he began to shout:

"Climb down, Mr Christy! Climb down and don't tempt Providence! You will hurt yourself and none of these bloodthirsty gawpers, who'd relish even a public execution outside the courthouse, will give you anything. Climb down, for Christ's sake, climb down!"

Ernesto greeted the grandpa with a salute, shifted onto the other toe and went back to minding his own business.

The old man slowly approached the rope, which hung down alongside one of the supporting poles, and then without a trace of anger began jerking and shaking it, all the while repeating his demand that the magician stop being foolish and climb down.

Several neighbours of the troublemaker started admonishing him. Antony and the major, anxious to prevent an accident, rushed up to him, but before they could intercept the hand of mockery or madness, the balancing pole carried by the magician had fallen and was followed by the poor magician himself, who with a cry of dismay came crashing down head first.

RAPACIOUS ONLOOKERS

"Saints alive!" So exclaimed several people who, taking Ernesto for more of a fool than he actually was, supposed that this hair-raising fall was part of the performance, and began a round of applause that sounded derisory in the circumstances.

Antony was compelled to box the ears of several giggling adolescents in order to infuse a proper understanding of what was going on. The major was forced to press his stick into service as the only instrument with which to bridle asses.

OLD HABITS DIE HARD

Learning the truth of what had happened and being encouraged by this example, the townsfolk set upon the old codger. Declaring him a shameless wretch they gave him a thrashing across the back and rump.

Indeed there was nothing left for him to do but turn tail and scurry off.

When an opportunity presented itself for the old man to get away, he broke into a run and dashed towards Boilermakers, the name of the upper gate, where there was a parking area for waggons. Eager in their condemnation of his error, the people ran after him to this spot. To this spot and no further! No further, because turning back at the aforementioned gate is an ancient custom of the town, one that is even maintained during Christian funerals.

THE MAGICIAN GETS THE BETTER OF PAIN

It took a long while for the crowd around Ernesto to disperse. The fallen magician could be seen picking himself off the ground, lifting up a painfully contorted face. He was a picture of misery. Nonetheless he turned down offers of assistance from Mr Hussey's elbow and the support of the major's walking stick.

From past feats of prowess, when he had wielded his pole above the town with a flourish, the magician had accumulated pride, and this pride enabled him to stand erect and walk off without so much as a glance to left or right. He made it to the waggon, through the open doors of which it was possible to observe Catherine Hussey, weeping bitter tears into her headscarf.

VULTURES GATHER ROUND THE CORPSE

Thunder pealed, flashes of lightning crisscrossed the heavens, but none of this stopped people from rushing out of their houses and hurrying to the square and Ernesto's rope. From the more curious came questions about what happened, while others responded:

"The magician's lost his life."

"The magician's lost all movement."

"Come off it! Haven't you heard? He's lost an ear just like Canon Gruntley!"

"He took a knock. Why was he such a chump? I mean, who sent him shinning up ropes? Why did he go climbing up there?"

"You know what, we'll collect a few coppers among ourselves and buy him a hen. He can make himself soup. This is the stuff they give to women in childbed. Great healing powers are hidden inside it."

"Goes without saying, dear neighbour. Only we don't hold with these whip-rounds. You'd just love to make a few purchases on our behalf, wouldn't you. You'd have a whale of a time."

"Bless my soul and upon my life, it's all true! It really happened! He's landed himself in it, and it was his back that felt the landing."

Talking in this way and that, panic-stricken and prattling, the people jostled each other with elbows and knees. There was such a crush of bodies that the women started howling and squealing in a manner normally heard round the waggons at harvest time. Such was the mêlée that the agitated countenance of the mayor rose above the throng, which had squeezed him out of its midst. Meanwhile the crowd trod on the doctor and squashed the constable, who was brandishing a firearm at the end of a right arm bare from the loss of a coat.

THE VOICE OF REASON

"If I am now speaking to you, Major," explained Antony, "it is mainly because I would like to hear once more the gentle voice of reason. I am afraid that this crowd of sympathisers has taken leave of its senses and is talking gibberish. I used to know some verses suitable for recitation in times of turbulence and trouble. I regret to say that I have not been able to retain in my memory more than a few words that run like this:

Run away, embrace escape –

You don't happen to know how it goes on?"

"No," came the rejoinder from Hugo, "but I dare say the canon does."

"Perhaps," the master agreed, "but he isn't present and this places his knowledge beyond use. But did you notice, Major, the way in which punishment strides one step behind the offence? The canon has a split ear, because he committed an act of treason, and Ernesto has sustained a bruising in the region of his pelvis. The huge blade-shaped bones in this region of the body form the pelvic girdle; whenever they are pushed against one another through a fall or blow, the agony follows of which we are witnesses. These are the wages of sin, the touch of heaven's fiery wrath."

"If you ask me," replied the major, "accidents in this square seem to fill you with satisfaction. You seem to approve of them."

"Most certainly not. I forgave the priest and wish no harm upon him," said Antony. "Even so the way one thing leads to another fills me with wonder. It all signifies a truly startling wisdom. You should take this to heart, Major. It serves both as example and cautionary tale."

SIMPLE SOULS

Anna did not see the magician fall. Before the performance began, when she had collected and counted the money, she took a milk jug and headed for Godwin's farm, her fist curled round the handle and her thumb pointing skywards.

This farm lies about twenty minutes from the town square, and can be reached more quickly if you run and have good legs and a lot of puff. Anna moved on without any premonition of disaster to come. She walked through the town, along the main road, through a copse and across a meadow, through a courtyard and at last stood on the threshold of the stables, where the farmer was twirling his moustache and the farmer's wife, anger written on her features, was gripping a pail between her knees, milk streaming into it from the udder.

Anna greeted them and, coins clinking in her pocket, she asked for a mugful of milk.

"Where did you get that idea?" asked the farmer's wife. "There's no milk for sale here. We wouldn't have enough for ourselves, not even if the size of the udder was twice what it is this year. That's what comes from a failure of the fodder harvest and hardly a clump of clover. We barely make ends meet in here, young lady. Why don't you try the cottagers. It's the land of plenty over there."

With these words the farmer's wife got up from her stool and carried the milk into the cellar.

The farmer nodded in agreement, but no sooner had his wife gone out than he grabbed the jug from Anna and running into the kitchen scooped up a potful of cream. The skin, which was certainly more than a finger thick and shaped like a crescent moon, hung over the side of the jug and dribbled cream.

"Here's your milk now, little miss," said the farmer, handing Anna her jug. "Come tomorrow after nine. That's when we're not so busy. We can have a little chat together."

The farmer put great emphasis into these last words. However, scarcely had they left his lips before he was hurrying into the house. He ran off, flinging himself in the direction of the milk pail with a single bound. There he plunged his lips into the white cream, the better to pretend that he'd drunk everything that was missing.

BACK TO TOWN

Anna returned home without any sense of agitation and passed the spot where the terrible incident occurred in an almost peaceful state of mind. Seeing the crowd gathered in front of Ernesto's green house, she supposed that some wretch had taken umbrage at the brevity of the performance and that people had assembled in order to ask for their money back. Such lamentable practices were common enough and were the main reason why the waggon wiped the dust off its wheels and set out on a new pilgrimage.

"Look what we have here," said Anna, walking through the crowd which had fallen silent. "No one complaining anywhere. What can be going on?"

Then she walked up the three steps and opened the door.

ADVICE FROM ANNA

The magician was lying flat on his stomach with his breath coming slowly and regularly. His face was no paler than at other times, he had full control of his limbs and he dwelt in the land of the living.

Taking in everything that had happened, Anna stood before Mrs Hussey, who was narrating the unfortunate incident between sobs, and said to her:

"My simpleminded opinion is that you are too given to crying. This is all stuff and nonsense. My relation is neither given to fatal leaps nor to tears which get on his nerves so. Kindly take Ernie's trousers and cap – even the mask if you like. I shall get into some short skirt and we'll organise a fresh performance, because there's a swarm of people outside. Get up, get dressed and get moving before they disperse."

"Well really," said Mrs Hussey, rising to her feet as the sobbing subsided, "I am a worthy woman of some substance who preserves her dignity. And you expect me to dress in trousers like these? Do you really think I would take part in fraud and subterfuge before the eyes of heaven and my own people? As far as I'm concerned, this performance of yours is based on pathetic and ridiculous deceit. I made haste to help when you were in dire straits, and you tucked into my hens and fish. I patched up your shirts and all those pieces of tat which do not deserve the name of garments, but now the cupboard is bare and there's nothing left to eat. My hands have grown used to honest toil. They will never again touch rags that reek from the sweat of forward rolls and greasepaint. Surely, sir, you have noticed that I cross myself every time you blaspheme and that I turn aside to avoid rubbing shoulders with this trollop. Good heavens, surely you don't think you're going to make me believe that this is some niece or sister of yours. I give thanks to God for the fact that I have grown accustomed to knitting stockings seated in front of an honest house. I will be sitting there again, because Antony is calling and gesturing for me to go back. I've seen him standing in front of the waggon with a troubled expression on his face two or three times. Looking pale and out of sorts. Ready to crush this little travelling box to pulp. Smash it to smithereens. Oh yes, you'd better watch out that he doesn't come here. Just go on thinking that I can be bound by the cramped spaces of a pigsty like this! Just go on thinking it! You're lily-livered and you're about to get your fingers burnt. Mr Hussey is standing just behind the door."

ERNESTO THE IRREPRESSIBLE

"Quite right," replied Ernesto. "You've wandered off from hearth and home in the interest of public order and you're a martyr to the cause, but now you can clear off home again or I will fetch my cane. I find my patience draining away with your rising virtue and once I get started I will teach you a lesson with a damnod good hiding. Go back where you came from and thank God for the fact that he let you become decent and respectable again without a thrashing."

ANNA'S WARDROBE

When Mrs Hussey was gone, Anna put on wonderful silk tights which suited her so well (because she was perfect about the thigh, petite about the knee, noble in the calf, slender of heel and charming in the foot. It was an anatomy for which a French King five hundred years ago would have gone so far as to wage a war, in which the people were wiped out and all the lands adjoining Spain left ravaged.) Fastening all her buttons and slipping into an attractive belt, on which two snakes were depicted with much art in the act of devouring one another, Anna stepped in front of the looking-glass and found herself pretty.

PERVERSE TASTES

"The Catchpole girl," she explained to the magician, "used to dance in the Ferdinand circus with a pear in her mouth. Some people considered her outlandish in her inventiveness and I can't myself imagine that such a thing really suited her. There is nothing better than a naked pink mouth without adornment. If there were no avoiding it, I would never choose a pear, but a rose. The custom is to clench it between your premolars and move it lightly back and forth."

OUR MOROSE CITIZENS

The town population, being of a gloomy disposition, prefers to stay in places struck by misfortune and mark them with various signs forever: trees, statuettes, paintings or small crosses, depending on the wealth of the community and the tastes of the local parish priest, who has to act in agreement with the secretary of the local beautification committee (and you can wager, sir, that at such solemn moments the secretary tends to keep his mouth shut, because the manners of a parish priest are those of a military marshal).

These unhappy places command respect, and therefore the people comported themselves nicely, forming a semicircle in the square. The discussion was about Ernesto and the rope. A strange and surprising range of opinions was to be found among them. No matter that they all viewed lying with contempt (because such a view was impressed on them in the schools and by august students of divinity) it seemed that some of them did not speak the truth. They dubbed Ernesto a little demon and a pathetic creature; they called him rude, smart alec and hobbledehoy; they said that he was knock-kneed, and then a moment later they said that he had arrived straddling a watermelon or that he was bowlegged. Some claimed that he was pretending to injury, others that he was dead and still others that he deserved two dozen lashes so that peace would return to the community.

GOOD THEATRE

While all this talk was going on, Anna left the waggon. Stepping onto the carpet spread out once more before her, she soon quietened everyone down. It was almost the depths of night. A hint of moonlight streamed down from the heavens above, gilding even the monsters below with a little grace. A glimmering drop of some sparkling radiance, which without a doubt had touched the mouths of angels, alighted on Anna's lips and awakened such a sense of sweetness and beauty that no one dared to breathe. The men kept their bodily functions in check and there wasn't a cough or a sneeze in the house.

In the wondrous light, which formed a moonkissed grotto in the darkness, Anna began to cross to and fro, emulating the manner of a tightrope walker. Despite the fact that she was walking on a ragged carpet, and despite the fact that Ernesto's rope was swinging in the wind fifty feet above her, nothing detracted from the greatness and supreme artistry of her steps.

FRANKLY AMAZED

"I defer to no one when it comes to piety," said one of the neighbours, "and I know that the square will not even collapse under the weight of cattle when the market is here (and at those times there's more heavy livestock than you can count). But mark my words, has not the place become a dark abyss above which, on a ray of sunlight, the thread used by the legendary weaver, a charming female apparition walks back and forth?

Yes indeed. That's how it should be. I could swear that the girl was walking on air.

I'd wager that it's no ordinary woman up there. Not a bit like my little Vera, who's a marvel with the household accounts but has flat feet."

AS IT'S MEANT TO BE

When Anna had done enough walking, she began some slight twists and turns which were reminiscent of the breakneck savagery of Ernesto's death-defying exercises. This only accentuated her beauty. She beat the drum, took frequent bows, laughed, flashed her eyes and poked fun at the people around, until she had them by the nose and eating out of her hand.

Eventually the gentlemen filled Ernesto's hat with plenty of money. There was no shortage of coppers in the take, but thank God for them. Every minnow has something of a fish in it.

THE ROOTS OF THE ART OF ACTING

"This wonderful achievement," said Antony, "stems from shamelessness and nothing else. Which, by the way, is something I approve of."

"I once saw a fireman on stage in the Champs-Elysées, who spent the whole performance pouring water from one bucket to another. Another time I was observing one of our emancipated actors. Once again he was pouring water, this time from glass to glass. Bless you, Major, it was not the same water, but both fireman and actor performed in the same grand manner. There is great ingenuity in the pouring of water, when it takes place not in private but in the public arena. (You and I, Major, who so often cause spillage between the bottle and the glass, are prevented from appreciating the beauty hidden in these actions by the fact that they occur on a daily basis and without interruption).

Well now, Major, Anna has shown us the mechanics of the human joint, the contraction and tightening of muscle fibres underlying the lifting of a leg, she has shown us that regular and unhurried breathing which swells the breast and, to the slightest of extents and in the most appropriate manner, even gives a gentle trace of movement to the stomach, and so she provides us with a delightful picture of simple existence and significant action such as lie at the root of theatrical performance. Here you see a person whose blood circulation leaves nothing to be desired, whose internal secretions are obviously sound, who opens up before our eyes the workings of human ligaments, all of which redounds to the glory of God, of whom it is said that He created the human body in His own image.

I owe it to the truth to declare," added Antony, taking off his hat, "that Anna has a firm rump with dimensions that are not excessive, that she is well-proportioned and has the organs of a thoroughbred."

"As to that," replied the major, "I'd say no doubt about it. You were quite right about the bodily functions too. I've found the same thing in soldiers. Legs more sturdy than beautiful, but the moment they took a forward step their boots were a sight for sore eyes. When we were on a march the sound of falling feet brought us out in song."

AN INCIDENT WITH A SLEEVE

Scarcely had he finished speaking before Anna made a final bow and wanted to slip on her coat, the sleeve of which was swaying about behind her back. It was a beautifully cut coat made from fine striped cloth, edged with Canadian sable (which for some years now has been difficult to find in the fur markets, because it has been squeezed out by an imitation which, alas, is nothing more than rabbit fur).

The major, having spotted the fluttering sleeve and noting the impropriety of Anna dressing like a maid in a hurry for the stagecoach, leaped down from the edge of the fountain and rushed to hold the coat, thereby providing Anna with relief during a strenuous moment. Then he offered her his arm and escorted her behind the waggon, where they spent five minutes in conversation together, discussing some age-old human emotions, having touched only fleetingly upon the subjects of exercise drill and marching.

When he arrived home, Master Antony discovered the door open and Mrs Hussey in the centre of the room.

"Just look what the cat's brought in!" she began with arms folded. "Where has the wanderer been straying? I've been to the swimming pool. The whole place is a mess and there's a blockage from twigs and leaves brought in by the river. What have you been doing, Antony?"

"So," began Antony, "Madam has come back for her things. Sort your stuff out, load up, get moving, get packing!"

"I came back," explained Catherine, "because I want to forgive you. Three days living in this unclean, deserted dwelling, with no food prepared for you and perhaps even sleeping rough, means that you have already received sufficient punishment for your faithlessness. I cannot be cross with you any longer, Antony."

"So much the better," came the reply from the master, "don't be cross with me, then. However, where my failings are concerned, I am incorrigible. Today I spotted a washerwoman, standing knee-deep in the Orsh. She was far uglier than Anna, but it was still clear to me that I couldn't mend my ways. Hence you should take your pots and pans and go to Ernesto. He's a model magician and a respectable husband."

"When I hear you talking like this," said his wife, slipping an old apron round her waist and scouring a pot, "it seems to me as if you made some arrangement with him to have me dragged off."

"You give me no alternative but to explain myself more clearly," said Antony. "Very well. You are a doxy and spent last night sleeping at Ernesto's. All right, I do not begrudge you your bodily pleasure, though it be the body of a bloated Gorgon, but I will punish you for the slanderous way in which you justify yourself."

"Hold your tongue," he added, when his wife wanted to reply, "I will permit you to stay but I cannot stomach your talk."

After which the master rolled up his sleeves and did as he'd hinted.

THE MAGICIAN OUT OF HUMOUR

Around midnight, when the inhabitants of the land of Nod are turning in their sleep, a lamp remained burning in Ernesto's waggon and the magician was awake. Silence reigned, The Green Maiden slumbered and no sound came from The Fourteen Helpers. Somewhere the rustic peace was being broken by the sound of slippers, in a way that was slightly reminiscent of Christmas, the time when your fortune is read from footwear as you throw it behind your back. The magician, however, was hearing without listening and staring into the fire. He was too incensed to sustain an appetite for jests. And now, in the manner of a connoisseur of justice, he was going over the events of recent days in his mind, looking for grievances, pouncing on wrongs and ferreting out the flagitious.

"Catherine Hussey," he opined, "is a swollen-headed grotesque. The canon is a dunderhead. Antony has received his comeuppance at home, but that major is a dangerous fellow!"

AN EXPEDITION

Despite all the pain he was in, he followed up these words by climbing out of the bed, slipping on his coat and shoes and taking his stick. He opened the door and went out before shutting and locking it. Then he started his journey, hanging on to the first thought that occurred to him.

He moved with care, feeling the rage throbbing inside him and the pain in the small of his back. Like a hobbling grouch he went along Brooke Street, Rampart Road and Cobbled Way, until he stood outside the major's house, where he sat down under an oak sapling. (There was an abundant supply of them, because a tree-lined avenue ran from the street to the door of the house, destined to grow tall and splendid as the major's taste dictated). Ernesto found it pleasant sitting there, and in order to keep his ferocity pure and prevent his anger from giving way to a mood of conciliation, he kept pinching his thighs. At the same time he looked up through the leaves at the stars, but as he was neither a man of piety nor one of letters, they conveyed no message to him.

THE DUEL

The doors finally opened at about three in the morning, before dawn had broken. Ernesto stood up and was gripped by a new fit of anger which made him set upon those who emerged, brandishing his stick. Anna and the major halted in their stride. Here was the magician charging at them without a bugler, a drummer or any military discipline. He thumped them, he pummelled and pounded them, until his strength was exhausted.

Anna was howling and repeating the major's name over and over again, but Hugo folded his arms and said:

"For God's sake, you mountain troll, don't tell me that you've brought your fork so that you can prick my calves. Are you planning to run me through with some sticklet used to stir fires?

Hell's teeth," he added, seeing part of the force from a blow land on Anna's back, "improve your aim or you'll do my lady an injury."

"Your lady!" exclaimed Ernesto, seizing hold of Anna by the hair, "Your lady! Have you taken leave of your senses?"

"No," replied Hugo, "for the simple reason that Anna is staying with me and you can be on your way."

The magician said that he would do as he wished. Anna looked at one man and then at the other. Having compared the splendid deeds of Ernesto with the idleness of the major, she opted for the former.

"Where the weaknesses of friends are concerned," she remarked, grasping the magician's hands, "leniency is called for. Let the major live. Do not finish him off."

Full of apprehension and wonder, she went off with Ernesto like a maiden propping up a hero of the Battle of Austerlitz. For the nobility that refrains from beating up a pauper has no access to the mind of a woman.

TRUE FRIENDSHIP

On the morning of the following day the canon straightened his bandage and made his way to the Lido Hussey.

"Gentlemen," he began after greeting the master life-guard and the major, "the ardour of friendship has driven me here to ferret you out. Are you in good health? Is everything well with you?"

"Well," came the response from Antony, "there cannot be a juster cause for complaint than mine, because you should know that Catherine has come back."

"Heaven's above," exclaimed the priest, "Frailty, thy name is woman. What can she be thinking? Why didn't you send her packing?"

Antony shrugged his shoulders and made no reply.

AN EPISODE CONCERNING PEOPLE WHO ARE UNBENDING AND THOSE WHO FORGIVE

There are some actions that in their severity go beyond the bounds of human understanding, just as there are decisions that exceed those limits in the forbearance which they show. Such behaviour does not conform to the common sense of the general public which, alas, is less developed than that of a donkey.

Do you know why this is? Someone completed an apprenticeship and became a chimney sweep. Now he carves matchboxes or birdcages with a fretsaw. He loves gardening, a pub full of people and a day full of sunshine. He is a man of integrity, and if his name is drawn out of the hat and he's appointed juror in a court where capital offences are tried, he'll always speak up for the forgiveness of trespasses and in his own way try to achieve justice in this wonderful world.

Another person, who has served a legal apprenticeship, will tearfully prepare the hangman's rope for a murderer and on the verge of fainting will spend the night from dusk till dawn with his mind fixed on the gruesome blade and the axe used by the miserable creature. This person is possessed by the truth of the law and he is just as mad as the do-gooder who forgave everybody for everything.

The harsh man of law and the righteous chimney sweep will not recognise how alike they are, not even if they meet playing skittles. But people will still point the same finger at them saying: look at those two madmen.

THE END OF THE EPISODE
After a free exchange of views in which all order and restraint were abandoned, master Hussey, the canon and the major were able to reach agreement with each other. But those who devote themselves to a new relative truth each week and feel at each moment a different vocation cannot understand them. The master, the man of God and the major are alone.

A FURTHER DISCUSSION

The silence which broke out in response to the canon's question flowed around them like the Orsh. The major removed his gloves and extracted a bottle from the cabinet.

"Anna has her marching orders," he said, "but Catherine is back on parade. Anna was a sight for sore eyes, Catherine is an eyesore, but still they resemble each other. I heard Anna sharing her opinions with Mrs Hussey. She called Antony far from gallant, Mr Gruntley a shallow bookworm, but her assessment where I was concerned was even worse, because she went off with Ernesto, assuming he'd got the better of me."

"You've been in some scrap with him?" asked Antony.

"The magician has a tiny spaniel," replied the major. "It gave me a thrashing this morning by one of the oaks in the avenue."

INCREDIBLE EVENTS

"Listen here!" exclaimed the canon as he put his glass down, "you put up with it. You did nothing to defend yourself." The man of God followed up these words with a clenching of his fist, coming as close to his two friends as he possibly could and launching into a tale of derring-do during his night-time adventure with Anna.

"When I realised," he said, "that these drunkards from The Green Maiden were getting through the window into the waggon, I was possessed by such a fit of temper that I would have bashed out the brains of those reprobates. My one regret is that my fist could neither cut nor pierce and was not heavy enough for the task."

"You did well," said Antony, "because you neither used your usual weapons nor cut these troublemakers down to size with a quotation. You and the major are sterling characters. But enough of this. Drink!"

When they'd emptied the glasses, the canon fell to thinking and then said:

"There are many facets to Antony's interest in this matter. Why did he not take precedence over the others in Anna's estimation?"

IT'S ALL OVER

"She chose me early on," commented the master, "but for just that reason it's now water under the bridge."

Not intending to speak any further about Anna, he then began to show the major a few exercises which would strengthen the left muscle of the heart. The canon opened a book, and when the master's demonstration was complete, even the major joined in the game, beginning to wriggle his wrists whilst maintaining a dignified silence throughout.

CATHERINE'S LIKES AND LOATHINGS

Mrs Hussey was standing among the willows at this time. Dark and sombre the Orsh flowed rapidly past her, birds she did not recognise hovered above her head, but Catherine herself was quiet. From the tower of St. Lawrence came the striking of the hour. After the bell had tolled, lunch came into the lady's mind, and as she turned her eyes ran over the rooves of the cabins and fixed on her husband's head.

"Look at that," she said with aversion, "Antony exercising his body in private. No doubt there's a nook where the canon has his nose in some tome; if I could hear him, I'd never be able to make out when he was starting to quote from a book and when he'd left off doing so. Those two follow their perversions with a passion. As for the major, stiffly hanging on his dignity with no fear of ridicule, there's not the slightest redeeming feature there, because only a madman attaches himself to a bygone era and makes no use of the present."

Her commentary complete, Mrs Hussey looked around her in all directions and then, as her gaze followed the line of the path which leads to the village of Coldstream and rises to a great height on the other bank of the river, she spotted a green waggon in the tow of a country jade. Ernesto was perched in the driver's seat cracking the whip. Anna was walking alongside the waggon leaning her palm against the side and the small dog was running along behind.

"Oh," she exhaled, feeling that she was bereft for a moment of all her self-assurance as a citizen, and wiped away a tear with the back of her hand. "Oh dear, oh dear, oh dear. How I long to conjure with fire and to wander the wide world juggling with those little round things. How wonderful to be thinking no more than three days ahead, to be peregrinating from one town to another.

How marvellous to plan a performance from beginning to end and then to repeat it day after day before people not one of whom, besides ourselves, knows what's going to happen next.

The lamps! The magic hat! The rope on high! Members of the audience, turn your eyes to me, for I am attired in Flemish tights and I support Ernie, because he is a frail little magician.

The splendour of it. The splendour of being endowed with a head of curls."

AFTERWORD

Vladislav Vančura wrote *Summer of Caprice* over the course of a few months in the summer of 1926. He was 35 at the time and living in a town near Prague called Zbraslav, where he had a medical practice. It is fair to say that medicine did not greatly interest him, given the fact that he passed on both the practice and its patients to his wife soon afterwards, devoting himself mainly to literature. He was hailed as the spiritual father of the young poets and painters grouped around Vítězslav Nezval, Jaroslav Seifert and Karel Teige. Vančura himself, however, wrote exclusively in prose, to be found in various literary and cultural journals, though later he also became a prominent figure in Czech film and theatre.

Summer of Caprice was his fourth book, written to some extent under the influence of Poetism, the Czech avant-garde movement which shortly after the first world war represented a sense of collective optimism, *joie de vivre* and a fascination with all things exotic. However, it is an unusual work when viewed in the context of his oeuvre taken as a whole. It contains none of the social dimension found in most of his novels and is built around a mosaic of short scenes that are not always clearly connected. Above all it is, as its sub-title states, a 'comic novel'. The humour in the story is realised through a mixture of linguistic dexterity and the situations in which its characters find themselves. It cannot be doubted that Vančura wrote this novella for fun, as an expression of the good times he was living through and indeed that the newly-formed Czechoslovak Republic was living through in the first half of the twentieth century.

Summer of Caprice was published only once in Vančura's lifetime, shortly after he completed it, and fell rather flat with the public. Another edition followed after the second world war, by which time Vančura was already dead. At that time the critics were often in two minds about the work. The author himself was valued mainly for his onetime allegiance to communism and his commitment to resisting fascism and this was also reflected in the appreciation of his works. Moreover, the peculiar richness and extreme difficulty of Vančura's language held up his translation into other languages, with the consequence that he remained known only in Czech literary circles.

The turning point came through Jiří Menzel's film version of *Summer of Caprice* in 1967, which brought the novel into the public eye. This is due to excellent acting performances depicting with passion and humour the atmosphere of a small and sleepy spa town, where three friends encounter one another around the swimming pool bereft of its public due to the 'capricious' June weather, 'caprice' being understood in the form of rain. The discussions between Antony (Antonín), the manager of the pool, Canon Gruntley (Roch) and Hugo, a retired major, which range over every possible subject-matter, each one doing so in his own way, are disturbed by the arrival of the magician Ernesto and his comely companion Anna. Their presence in the town and the acrobatic display in the evening provide the inhabitants of Krokovy Vary (Little Karlsbad) with a night to remember and disturb the quiet lives of the heroes of our story. None of them is able to resist the natural charms of Anna. The tragicomic love affairs which they enjoy with her bring about a no less tragicomic rupture in the relations between Antony and his wife Kateřina (Catherine). The upshot of this delightful farce is a return to what went before, the sleepy life of a small spa town and an empty bathing area where three friends reminisce over a glass of wine. They reminisce about what they have just lived through, even though they, like Catherine, know that while they might still muse over and dream of something new or even a different life, it is not something their own future has in store for them.

Like any adaptation, Menzel's film couldn't carry over into another genre what is a distinctive characteristic of the novel, namely its language. A similar problem confronts any translator. Vančura tells his story using very distinctive terminology, in which the colloquial mixes with the archaic, the metaphorical with the idiomatic, and truisms join neologisms in wandering digressions. Language is the unifying feature of the novel, in which a sophisticated richness of discourse contrasts with the more plebeian tones of the heroes of the tale. Those tones are skilfully disguised by the refined discourse of Major Hugo, the learning of Canon Gruntley and the hedonism and bon-vivant jollity of Antony, as well as the assiduous petit-bourgeois aspirations of his wife Catherine. And this contrast between refinement and rawness is the founding principle of the humour in *Summer of Caprice*. Several sentences have become part and parcel of common speech in certain situations, such as Antony's brief sigh in front of the thermometer in the bathing area where he says: *tento způsob léta zdá se mi poněkud nešťastným* ('Such a summer, seems to me, spells misfortune'). The extent to which such expressions are taken over into common parlance is evidently not something that can be captured in a translation.

Naturally a translation can relatively faithfully describe the situations in which the heroes of the tale find themselves, even though a question remains concerning how far the comic character is communicable. For example in the chapter entitled *Představení třetí* (The third performance) an old man, apparently somewhat the worse for wear, warns the acrobat Ernesto, who is walking the tight-rope, that he should climb down or risk a fall. Whereupon the old man persistently yanks on the rope, eventually causing one of the poles supporting Ernesto's rope to fall, after which the acrobat himself comes tumbling down. Doubtless this grandpa said to himself, as he fled from the square, that his warning had proved correct. A similarly glib excuse applies to the situation where cocky and ostentatious Antony searches for a simple explanation when he is caught red-handed by his wife with Anna in a changing-cabin of the bathing pool. Compare the way the moralising canon pluckily does battle with the drunken rustics who get inside the waggon he gate-crashed in pursuit of Anna. Most paradoxical of all in this respect is the behaviour of Major Hugo who never misses an opportunity to bring up his military past, but then receives a thrashing from Ernesto, who after his fall from the tight-rope is barely able to walk.

It can be said that Vančura presented in a fairly precise manner typical Czech characters, although that was evidently not the main drift of his works. Antony and Hugo see themselves as heroes, but only when they are in the company of a glass of wine. The divine is incessantly moralising, but when he is fleeing from Anna he even vandalises a street light in order to prevent anyone recognising him. As for Catherine, having decided to devote her life to the magician, in order to seek revenge over her faithless husband, she goes back to him for fear of being recognised by the small town burghers in the role of helper to Ernesto, a travelling trapeze artist and magician. Ernesto himself evokes a romantic longing for faraway places and foreign lands, which was a distinctive feature of the Czech poetic avant-garde in the 1920s. While poets and painters would dream of life under a wandering star, with exotic circuses and travelling waggons, their actual lives would be a far cry from it. In this respect they are just like Catherine, who watches the departure of Anna and Ernesto in their waggon from Little Karlsbad with a tear in her eye.

Although Vančura's work has been recognised as being hard to translate, the endeavour to make it accessible to readers from abroad is undoubtedly worthwhile. And this novel in particular deserves a wider readership, since it rightfully places Vančura in a long line of Czech authors, from Jaroslav Hašek through Bohumil Hrabal to Milan Kundera, who have the ability to use humour in order to convey serious things.

Jan Rubeš
Université Libre, Bruxelles

TRANSLATOR'S NOTE

People always know when they're reading a Vančura. They can recognise his experimental style from a few lines of text, where the archaic mixes with the innovative and a raw colloquialism somehow joins hands with a biblical quotation, enriching both.

Some have argued that this 'poetism in prose' is better translated by film than written text (it could be pointed out that Vančura himself was a film director). Certainly Vančura's work has been filmed very successfully (the present book was made into an internationally acclaimed film in 1969, under the oscar-winning director Jiří Menzel).

So should it be translated into prose at all? There is much to be said for making the effort. For one thing, it should not be forgotten that Vančura's strength lay not only in style but also in characterization, and a translation should at least be able to bring the strong characters of Rozmarné léto to life. Secondly, it is true that translation always changes the original, and that is bound to mean leaving some of the glory behind. But it also allows a work and even its distinctive style to flourish in a new environment. The consequences of putting a text into another language are never entirely negative. Thirdly, Vančura deserves a wider audience. That alone justifies the attempt at a translation, if not always the result.

Mark Corner

TRANSLATOR'S ACKNOWLEDGEMENT

In order to tackle this work I had to look to several people for advice and assistance, and I am very grateful to have this opportunity for thanking them. Professor Petr Bílek and Dr. Ondřej Pilný told me not to be put off by the charge that Vančura is untranslatable, and suggested useful reading. When I had a draft translation ready, Jana Branšovská, Dr. Richard Haas, Mary Hawker, Nigel Hawker, Mgr. Lucie Johnová, Dr. Šárka Kuhnová, Thomas Prentis, Professor Robert Pynsent, Jana Vrbová and Martin Janeček read it through and helped to make it better (though for its present failings they bear no responsibility whatsoever).

Above all my wife Lenka Cornerová Zdráhalová, as the biggest critic, was the greatest help. Particular thanks for her painstaking work in reading through and correcting this translation.

Mark Corner

Central European modern history is notable for many political and cultural discontinuities and often violent changes as well as many attempts to preserve and (re)invent traditional cultural identities. This series cultivates contemporary translations of influential literary works into English (and other languages) which have not been available to global readership due to censorship, the effects of Cold War or repetitive political disruptions in Czech publishing and its international ties.

Readers in English both in today's cosmopolitan Prague or anywhere in the physical and electronic world can thus become acquainted with works which capture the Central European historical experience and which express and also have helped to form Czech and Central European nature, humour and imagination.

Believing that any literary canon can be defined only in dialogue with other cultures, the series will bring proven classics used in Western university courses as well as (re)discoveries aiming to provide new perspectives in intermedial areal studies of literature, history and culture.

All titles are accompanied by an afterword, the translations are reviewed and circulated in the scholarly community before publication which has been reflected by nominations for several literary awards.

Modern Czech Classics series edited by Martin Janeček
and Karolinum Press

Published titles
Zdeněk Jirotka: Saturnin (2003, 2005, 2009, 2013; pb 2016)
Vladislav Vančura: Summer of Caprice (2006; pb 2016)
Karel Poláček: We Were a Handful (2007; pb 2016)
Bohumil Hrabal: Pirouettes on a Postage Stamp (2008)
Karel Michal: Everyday Spooks (2008)
Eduard Bass: The Chattertooth Eleven (2009)
Jaroslav Hašek: Behind the Lines. Bugulma and Other Stories (2012; pb 2016)
Bohumil Hrabal: Rambling On (2014; pb 2016)
Ladislav Fuks: Of Mice and Mooshaber (2014)
Josef Jedlička: Midway Upon the Journey of Our Life (2016)
Jaroslav Durych: God's Rainbow (2016)
Ladislav Fuks: The Cremator (2016)

In Translation
Bohuslav Reynek: The Well at Morning
Ludvík Vaculík: Czech Dreambook
Jan Čep: Short Stories
Viktor Dyk: The Pied Piper